Abroad - Cuernavaca, Mexico

A Novela of Adventure

Merideth Rose Cleary

Text copyright ©2013 by Merideth Rose Cleary
All rights reserved
No part of this book may be reproduced, stored in a retrieval system, or transmitted by any means, electronic, mechanical, or otherwise, without written permission from the author.
This is a work of fiction. Names, characters, places, or incidents are products of the author's imagination or are used fictitiously. Any resemblance to actual persons, living or dead, business establishments, events, or locations is entirely coincidental.

ISBN: 1497575001
ISBN 13: 9781497575004

Table of Contents

Dedication

I would like to thank my mother, Elizabeth Cleary, without whose support and encouragement I never would have written this book; my father, Lonny Renfroe; my brother, Shay Cleary, for his constant support; and my nephews, Ian (*aka* Jesse) and Colin (*aka* Jake); and my niece, Elise Cleary. Special thanks to my aunt, Jeannie Dellinger, and her husband David; and most of all to my li'l Sophia Rose, who I hope will travel further than I ever have in this great, big, wondrous world of ours! Much love, peace, and aloha to all I have not mentioned.

Introduction

Not so long ago my nephew, who, it is relevant to note, is being brought up Catholic, pulled me into his closet because he had a very important question he wanted to discuss. I thought to myself, "What perplexing question could be on this ten-year old's mind that would require a private discussion in his closet?"

Now, mind you, my nephew is and has always been a very pensive individual who, at his very young age, amazes me with his thoughtfulness, wit and intelligence, so I was ready for anything. We squeezed into the closet, which was packed full of items ranging from his Catholic school uniforms hanging nicely from their hangers to the life-size stuffed dog on roller skates in the corner that I had bought for him when he had turned six years old, to his soccer uniforms, bins full of shoes, and all the other random items one may find in a closet. He closed the door and it became very dark. At this moment I realized how privileged I was to be an aunt and to have this young soul asking my advice about anything, considering that at ten he could explain the speed of light, a concept I still struggle with, to be honest.

So as to not seem like a looming figure in the dark, I knelt down so we could talk face to face without being able to see each other in the pitch black of the closet.

"Aunt Melissa," he said in a muffled voice, and I could tell he was facing the opposite direction, maybe talking into one of his pairs of school pants, so I turned him to face me.

"I am right here Jesse, what is it?"

"Aunt Melissa...." Reaching out, he accidentally nearly stuck the end of his little finger in my eye. "Oh, sorry, Aunt Melissa," he said.

"That's okay," I replied gently, lowering his arm with mine.

"Aunt Melissa," he said for the third time.

"Yes, Jesse, what is it?" I asked patiently, almost chuckling at the whole scenario. Now, as mature and developed as he was, I was pretty sure he was going to ask me a question that had to do with what he should get his mom for her birthday, or maybe he was going to ask what I wanted for my birthday, or most likely he was going to tell me what he wanted for his birthday, which for any ten-year old is definitely a conversation worthy of dragging a family member into a dark closet and nearly poking their eye out to discuss.

"Well, I have a problem," he said.

That one statement opened my mind to an array of different possibilities. "Was someone bullying him at Catholic school?" I thought to myself. "Please do not let it be some disgruntled bully with braces and head-gear taking his lunch money every day." I mean, I never had to wear head-gear or braces, and I genuinely feel bad for anyone who has, but let's admit it, folks, those things are just plain creepy-looking no matter what. Then I thought, "Was it bed-wetting?" You see, this is why I was glad I had not had kids yet – what do you do with a bed-wetting ten-year old anyway? Or maybe he was already considering becoming a vegetarian. He did read a lot, and he had seemed to be avoiding his hot dog at lunch earlier that day.

So, all ready to throw out all the reasons why it is not that big of a deal to bed-wet at ten years old – I mean, I dated a guy once in my early years of college who would get so drunk he would wet himself at least twice a month. Now, that is a problem worth discussing in private, if you ask me. Probably best not to use that particular example with my ten-year old nephew, but I could tell him how I myself went through a vegetarian phase in college until I realized I missed a nice, juicy red steak every now and again, not to mention going to the zoo without feeling like a total hypocrite.

But before I could offer any of my wisdom, Jesse said, in the most innocent of voices, "Well, Aunt Melissa, the problem is I want to be a priest someday, but I also want to get married someday – and I can only do one of them. What should I do?"

Okay, can I just say that that school is doing their job! Holy Shit! I mean literally, *HOLY* shit! I mean – what ten-year old asks that question? At ten I was probably debating whether I wanted to go with shoelaces or Velcro or just stick with jellies and not even worry about shoes that fasten. Or I was debating which My Little Pony was the coolest, Bubbles or Cotton Candy? Or most likely I was imagining myself as a dancer on tour with Madonna (my idol at ten years old) traveling to New York or the Caribbean, training with her to dance in next video….

And then it hit me… and before I could stop the words from coming out of my mouth I told him, "Jesse, I think that before you make that decision you need to travel some. See the world a bit. See how people live in other places, and then make the decision."

"Hmmmm, travel?" he asked.

"Yes," I said. "You know, your aunt Melissa did a couple study abroad programs in college and honestly, it is very important to learn about other cultures."

"Ohhhh," he said. "Other cultures…."

"Yeah… other cultures," I repeated.

As we sat for a moment I did have to acknowledge in my mind that he honestly would make an AMAZING priest. First off, he already was a tad bit holier than thou – I mean, one time he actually almost called 9-1-1 because he saw the neighbor kid littering, no lie. The poor neighbor kid threw his popsicle stick in the grass at his own house and Jesse ran inside screaming, "Call the police! Call the police! Brad littered!"

You try explaining to a kid that, yes, some activities in the world are illegal, but you don't have to call the police into the situation because there are some illegal actions that society just frowns on instead of actually doing anything about, like recreational pot smoking, pirating movies, or the all time classic, removing the tags from a mattress. These subtle rules of life are not easy to explain to an overly curious tween and maybe, just maybe, it was for that reason my instincts were to advise him to travel. Get out of the box. See the world. Go to Amsterdam for Pete's sake! Ride a bike along the Amstel river with Brad from the old neighborhood you grew up in together… while drinking an Amstel Light for that matter. Break away from the pack.

After a minute of deep contemplation Jesse said, "That is good advice, Aunt Melissa… to travel."

He then paused. "But not to the desert, right, Aunt Melissa?"

God, I love kids, they say such random things. "Why not the desert?" I asked Jesse.

"Because the desert has tarantulas and I *reeeeeeeaaaallllllly* don't like tarantulas."

I chuckled, pulled him in for a hug, and said, "There are lots of places with no deserts, like Ireland, New York, Indonesia, Thailand...."

"Cool...Thailand...." responded Jesse with an airy tone in his voice.

Why the advice to travel so easily fell out of my mouth still baffles me to this day, but I feel that even though I still have trouble grasping the speed of light, I do believe I gave my little nephew good advice. Nothing will teach one about the subtle rules of life better than delving into every part of it as you can, and what better way than breaking out of your bubble and traveling. Now, as I sit and write this from my home in Hawaii, which in many ways is much like a foreign country, I have a baby girl on the way (in a matter of weeks!) and to her I would say, "Travel, little girl! See the world! Start with studying abroad. It is one of the best ways to literally live in another country and not just be a tourist touching the surface for a week or two. Then, if you can't get rid of the travel bug, find work abroad. Buy a home abroad, or marry a foreigner, and if it doesn't work out, get rid of the dude – but make sure to get that dual citizenship!"

And as I deal with the challenges of being a mother-to-be, maybe, just maybe, I should have advised Jesse to become a priest! *Ha ha!* Or maybe after he travels a bit he will still decide to become one, if this book does not scare him into the priesthood first.

Chapter One

I was 22 years old and had changed majors more often than Taylor Swift changes boyfriends, and maybe I was just as lost as my nephew, because I was definitely searching for my path high and low. All I can say is – my *poooor* mother! After, as I said, numerous changes in majors, I thought I had finally settled on elementary education. That was until the first time I actually observed a fourth-grade classroom as part of one of my prerequisite classes to start student teaching and graduate.

And this is *exactly* why I would advise my soon-to-be-born daughter and my nephew to travel before jumping headlong into some career, say as a priest… or a teacher. Okay, priesthood I guess is more of a calling than a career, but teaching fourth grade seems to require pretty much all the requirements of a priest – besides the celibacy part: patience, restraint, saintliness, you know what I'm saying.

So, after sitting and observing a classroom for ten minutes and seeing one little boy go and sharpen his pencil at the sharpener and then proceed to dump all the shavings in his hand, walk straight up to another student – an innocent girl he most likely had a crush on – and dump the pile of shavings on her head, which prompted her to stand up and push him so hard he fell on another innocent student minding his own business, I began to have doubts. Then the girl began to cry as she tried to shake the shavings out of her hair while the two boys got into it. All the while the teacher was trying to figure out how to break this all up without laying a finger on any of the students. The rest of the students just sat there either snickering at the whole event or completely baffled with their mouths hanging open. And I am sitting there thinking, "Hmmmm… I have only been in here for ten minutes. Can I picture myself dealing with this every day… for seven to eight hours a day… for the rest of my professional career?"

Well, needless to say, it did not take me long after charging out of that classroom before I whipped out my phone, called my mom and said, "Mom, I think I need to change my major… again."

To be honest, I think she was actually relieved because she never seemed to be that gung-ho about me becoming a teacher in the first place. I guess a mom knows her kids better than they may know themselves sometimes. Anyway, that is when I decided, as a senior in college, to study abroad in Mexico.

I had already taken three classes of beginner Spanish as part of my general studies, and when I thought about it all, I realized I was not quite ready to be a teacher just yet. I really liked the idea of still being a student – and of learning how to say words, even the most basic ones, like apple and table and lamp, in another language. It made me feel like a kid again, and I knew that after the classroom observation experience I had I was not quite ready to commit myself to anything quite yet. So, I did some inquiring with one of my Spanish teachers and found out that there was a semester program in a city in Mexico called Cuernavaca, which, after a little research, I learned was nicknamed "The City of Eternal Spring" because of its warm, consistent climate and lush vegetation.

Now, that sounded pretty awesome to me being that another cold, bitter, unforgiving Minnesota winter was looming, and if I hustled with filling out the required paperwork (immunizations, applying for the passport/student visa, travel insurance, etcetera) I could miss that winter and spend it improving my Spanish in the City of Eternal Spring. I was in!

So, what could be better than having a friend along for your first extended period of time in another country? Well, we will get to the answer of that later, but the point is, a friend of mine, Kelly, who I had met in one of my beginner Spanish classes, decided that she wanted to do the program as well, so we jumped through all the hoops together in applying, which did seem easier and more fun than doing it all solo. When it came to the question of living together (with a host family) we agreed that we would make great roommates, and so we requested the option of rooming together.

Before leaving I of course did more in-depth research before getting on the plane, and learned that Mexico is also called the United Mexican States (of which there are 31) and Cuernavaca is the capital and largest city of the state of Morelos. The name Cuernavaca means "surrounded by or close to trees," but was given its nickname, "Eternal City of Spring," by a world explorer named Alexander von Humboldt in the nineteenth century. He named it this because it is situated in a tropical region, yet its temperatures normally always fall in the 70's – so it always feels like spring. It is located on the southern slope of the Sierra de Chichinautzin mountains, where in the morning hours warm air makes its way up the mountains from the valley below and in the late afternoon, cooler air flows down from the higher elevations, making it close to perfect – not too humid while still allowing for flowers and fruits to grow, surrounded by waterfalls and fresh-water springs.

It seemed like a fairy tale for someone who had spent the majority of her life either freezing during the winter or battling the insane humidity of the Minnesota summers, which also included fighting off swarms of mosquitoes and gnats, I may add. I swear, if Minnesota could be diagnosed with a disorder, it would most likely be bipolar/ADD because between summer and winter come fall and spring where one day it is 70 degrees and the next it is 30 degrees and then the following day back to 70 degrees. The flowers start to bloom one day and then the next day a bitter frost kills everything. It starts to snow so you get your snow shovel back out, and then the next day everything is muddy and slushy because the temperature decides to shoot back up to 50 degrees and so forth. It is enough to drive a girl batty, I tell you!

One early January day, as I was packing my bags and getting ready for the trip, I looked out my dorm room window and I could see fellow students making their way through the snowy drifts as they headed to this class or that class. They trekked slowly across campus, looking much like arctic explorers as they tried to avoid slipping on the black ice that lay hidden underneath the snow while at the same time walking as fast as possible to avoid frostbite (and mind you, the University of Minnesota's campus is one of the largest in the nation, so it literally is a trek).

The thing you don't know if you have not attended the University of Minnesota in the winter is that underneath all those layers of scarves and Gore-Tex jackets with fur-lined hoods and long underwear and hats and mittens and snow boots is a student who is swearing like a sailor and cursing the cold, bitter howling wind and the god responsible for creating it, and his or her own parents for having raised him or her in this ridiculously bitter cold state anyway. And they do this the whole way to class. Only you cannot hear his or her cries of complete frustration because the voices are muffled by the very exact same bitter howling wind and layers of scarves and Gore-Tex jackets with fur-lined hoods, making it impossible for their voices to travel past their cold, red, almost frozen noses. I know this because I was one of those poor souls for five years! So needless to say, waterfalls, eternal spring, perfect climate, tropical fruit and flowers? COUNT ME IN!

Chapter Two

I have to say I barely remember the day I left for Mexico, except for the fact that is was cold and snowing. What I remember very vividly, though, was arriving in Mexico. The warmth of the air seemed to immediately start healing my cracked skin (another lovely attribute of living in a cold state like Minnesota – dry, chapped skin). I never realized skin should actually feel so soft and smooth. Mine had been cracked so long I guess I was just used to it. I also felt the warmness of the people as we got off the plane and waited for our bags. There was a joy and youthfulness in the people, and I began to wonder if they were just happier in general because they were warmer.

This is no lie, I once had a really weird dream that a friend of mine was planning to commit suicide and when I asked her why, she said it was because she was just so damned cold. This must have been right in the middle of one of the bitter Minnesota winters I described earlier, and my mind was just processing how I was going to go on winter after winter dealing with it. Needless to say, my friend did not commit suicide, but still – is not living while suffering a slow form of suicide anyway? Anyhow, I digress.

The bus ride from the airport in Mexico City to Cuernavaca was a delight to all the senses. All the sights, smells and sounds of the birds, flowers and people we passed was sort of like watching the movie *Avatar* in 3-D. Everything felt so bright and illuminated compared to the greyness of the Minnesota winter I had left behind. It was only a 30-minute ride, but maybe that was for the best – one does not want to overwhelm the senses too much!

Because we were arriving in the evening, we were dropped off at the homes we were all to be living in for the next couple months. This way we had a chance to meet our host families, unpack, have a shower, eat some dinner and get ready for orientation at the school the following day. The bus dropped Kelly (you remember Kelly, my friend who was also doing the program) and me off at the home we would be staying at, and right away Elena, our housemother, greeted us. She was a thin woman who had a very beautiful face and a chic haircut. She worked at Macy's in the cosmetics department, we were told, and definitely had a sense of style and class to her. We hugged, and in our rudimentary Spanish told her how beautiful everything was in Mexico and how wonderful it was to meet her. She said very sweetly that we would have lots of time to get to know each other, but first things first, let's get settled in a bit. She walked us around what we realized was the main house where she lived.

Behind it was a cottage, separate from the house, where Kelly and I would be living. It was quaint and adorable and had a balcony one could go up to, and let me just tell you, it was *PERFECT!* Beautiful, lush plants and trees surrounded it, giving off a smell that was so sweet and divine I could have sat there and just smelled the air all night. Beautiful flowers and palm trees painted the backdrop of our little cottage where bright, colorful singing birds plopped themselves on the branches of bird-of-paradise plants so it looked as though the plants were actually singing. It was like a scene from *Snow White*, except Snow White would be Mexican and the blue birds would be brightly colored parakeets. And to think I could have been starting to student teach fourth grade during one of the coldest months of the year in one of the coldest states in the world had God not stepped in and placed that little pencil shaving dropper of an angel into my life at the right exact time, prompting me to do a complete 360˙ with my life and get on a plane to a place that could be described as a tropical paradise.

As we entered the little cottage, we were both delighted to see two little beds, two little dressers with a pitcher of clean water set on a tray on a night stand in between the bed, and two clean glasses. We had been advised to not drink the water from the tap, so we got used to being sparing about the water. We unpacked our suitcases, both giddy and in awe at how beautiful and warm it was outside and that for the next couple of months we would make this little haven our home.

Chapter Three

Elena invited us in for dinner at about eight o'clock. She had a cook named Alita, who was probably in her early 70's. She was short with greying hair and she had a disheveled look to her. She did not speak a word of English and seemed almost deaf, so for the most part Kelly and I just nodded at her with big smiles when she would bring the food, repeating "gracias, gracias" over and over, and she would nod back with an even bigger smile and then we would nod at her even more emphatically and so on. Apart from that we pretty much let Elena do the communicating with her.

By the time dinner was served, Elena had smoked a cigarette and was about to light up another one. I did notice that at the airport many people had been smoking as well, and I realized that perhaps the idea that smoking was bad for you had not caught on in places outside of the United States; a friend who had traveled to Europe said the same thing – everybody smoked there – and a lot. Of course North Americans are dying left and right from heart disease, stress, and diabetes, so it seems that if one thing doesn't kill you another will. I was just glad Elena kept the window near the table open, allowing the smoke to waft out instead of letting it just hang out over the dining room table.

As we chatted I began to develop a theory that the reason Elena smoked was because she was a widow and it was out of loneliness for her Enrique who had passed away several years prior that she did it. She did have a son though, Enriquito (little Enrique), who was anything but little. She showed us a picture of him. He was in his 30's, tall, dark and very handsome. She said we would be meeting him at some point (*dot dot dot*)!

When Alita came out to serve the first meal I was happy as a clam in mud. REAL Mexican food! A wonderful beef broth with a hint of jalapeno pepper and cilantro – it even had bones and all. Well, Kelly was not as happy. And then I remembered that Kelly was a strict vegetarian because she had made a big huff about it all as she filled out the paperwork which had a spot on it to mark if you were vegetarian or not – so she wrote in bold letters that she was a STRICT VEGETARIAN! NO MEAT! Well, let me say, this was the meatiest beef soup I had ever had – not your typical Campbell's in a can with little chunks of some type of brown matter that we are asked to believe is beef. I think in Mexico they use the whole damn cow and that is why it tastes so damn good, pardon my French. After watching Elena squeeze lime into her soup I did the same, and I could barely hear Kelly's voice in my ear whispering, "This has meat in it. There is beef in this."

I replied, "I know, and if you squeeze lime in it, it is *DEEE-LISH!*"

She gave me a nasty look and said to Elena in her beginner level Spanish, "Elena, lo siento pero esto tiene carne y no como carne" ("Elena, I am sorry but this has meat in it and I don't eat meat").

Elena looked at the soup and said, "¿Carne?" ("Meat?"), and Kelly replied "Sí, carne. Yo soy una 'vegetarian'" ("Yes, meat, and I am a vegetarian").

Kelly then turned to me and asked how to say "vegetarian" in Spanish. I shrugged my shoulders and guessed, "Vegetarian-o?"

"Ahhhhh…" Elena said as she nodded that she understood, and then she snapped her fingers while calling out Alita's name.

Alita came dashing in with her usual disheveled look. "¿Sí, Señora?" she asked as if she were a soldier in the military and Elena was her commander. Elena spewed out a long sentence in one breath, pointing at the soup and making other gestures, and this is when I realized I really had a long way to go until I mastered Spanish. She spoke so fast I could not make out one word she said except "carne."

Sure, I could understand my instructor at the University of Minnesota, who purposely spoke so slowly it was as if she were working with mentally challenged students, which actually is what we were. When one has not developed the vocabulary and the grammar in another language to understand what is being said, I would say they are challenged mentally – which is how I felt for the next three months. Numberless times in those months I would just sit there nodding along as Spanish thwarted me at that damned speed of light, and just when I would think that maybe I got one word, before you know it the person blasting the Spanish at me would be sitting there waiting for me to respond to them.

Then I would realize they had asked a question and either I could nod my head for "Sí" or shake it for "No" or… maybe it was an open ended question that could not be answered with just a yes or no, which was the majority of the time. This is one of those experiences that forces you to realize you cannot B.S. your way through some situations in life. Most of them, yes, but some of them, no; and knowing what is being said to you and how to respond is one of those situations you have to get real in to survive.

So, after Elena finished her spew of Spanish, Alita took Kelly's plate, repeating over and over, "Lo siento, Señorita. Lo siento, no carne, no carne."

To which Kelly said, "Sí, no carne – vegetarian-o, no carne." Alita then scuttled into the kitchen while I continued enjoying the soup with lime and the bread and salad along side it (which was really just some greens and a vinaigrette dressing), which Kelly began to devour along with her bread. We had not eaten since the plane ride, and before we knew it, after some clanking around in the kitchen, Alita came out with another bowl of hot steaming soup. Kelly looked pleased until Alita set the bowl down and we both realized that she brought out chicken soup – bones and all with a nice quartered lime on the plate. So the same scenario repeated, where in her slow, beginner Spanish, Kelly explained to Elena that this soup has chicken in it – which is meat.

Elena, semi-frustrated once again, snapped her fingers and called Alita back out to the dining room. This time I really listened, and I think what she said was, "She says this one has meat in it, too." Alita looked completely confused and said something to Elena in very fast Spanish with a dash of frustration. Elena then said to Kelly, "Alita says that chicken is not meat. Beef is meat, but chicken is not, it is just a chicken."

To which Kelly replied, "Yes, chicken is meat, in the United States chicken is meat and so is pork." So Elena translated into Spanish what Kelly said, and Alita began to nod her head in pure frustration while muttering something. This was when I realized I must begin to listen *verrryyy* carefully to what was being said around me, because I swear I thought Alita muttered something along the lines of, "Well, we are not in the United States, are we, Señorita?" which Elena translated as, "She will bring you something without meat in it, don't worry." Five minutes later Alita returned with a plate of rice and beans and some more salad and bread and set it down with a little clank and said, "No carne, Señorita."

Elena then lit a cigarette and asked that Alita start the chocolate caliente (hot chocolate), and Kelly picked at her plate, eating only the rice and salad. That night as we went to bed Kelly said what I knew she was going to say. "Those beans were cooked with meat."

"I know," I responded. "Maybe tomorrow she will get it right," I added, knowing that she most likely would not and that Kelly might be eating a lot of salad and bread for the next three months.

Chapter Four

That night as I lay there I thought about how amazing this experience was going to be, and how envious my friends back in Minnesota would be if they could be here. I mean, I was in Mexico for crying out loud! While those dopes were back freezing their tails off in Minnesota, I was about to embark on one of the most amazing experiences of my life. I imagined traveling to the ocean and playing in waterfalls surrounded by the sweet smells of the flowers and fruits. Back in Minnesota, the only smells during the winter were of exhaust coming from cars that were stuck in snow banks or burnt rubber from tires that had been dug so far into the icy ground that they would almost start to burn. "*Ha!* What dopes!" I thought again.

And just as I was getting cocky about how smart I was to have jumped on this amazing opportunity… it started: Kelly began to snore.

At first it was a light snore, but it quickly grew into a loud grumbling that would stop every now and again and then, just when I would think she was done, she would literally erupt into a new snore, a new, mutated snore that was worse than the last. Either it was louder or more violent than the one prior, or it would turn into a soft whistle. It was like listening to opera; it evoked emotions that I can't explain. I was *sooooo* tired from the flight and the excitement of the trip, and of course the next day we had to be up bright and early for the first day of orientation. And damn it all, because of her snoring I could not hear the soft breeze from outside, and I was thirsty but did not want to drink the water so much as pour it over Kelly's head, and this lasted until about four in the morning, reaching the point that I almost went and slept outside.

So the next morning when Kelly awoke all bright-eyed and bushy-tailed and began to go on and on about how well she had slept with the warm tropical breeze, all I could do was say, "I know." I know you slept well, the whole neighborhood knows you slept well, Montezuma could hear you snoring in his tomb for crying out loud. But, I did not say anything more – I was too damn tired. And so we went into Elena's for some breakfast. I was so tired, I felt like a truck had run over my head. I was relieved when Alita brought the coffee out. Our breakfast was the same every day – cereal, a banana, a glass of fresh squeezed orange juice and a cup of coffee – no meat.

Because I was in my early twenties I was able to bounce back rather quickly from the lack of sleep the previous night, and I hoped and prayed that it was a one-time snoring session – or maybe just a once in awhile thing – and I jumped right into the orientation day. We met teachers and other students, we were taken on a tour of the school and then of the city, and we were given our class schedules. Classes began the following day. That night we ate dinner with the school as part of the tour, and after returning to our cottage and saying hello to Elena we both took showers and were ready for bed early, or at least I was.

Kelly was chatty, and she went on about how exciting everything was. I thought that maybe if I fell asleep before her I would be in such a deep slumber from being so tired that I would not wake if she began to snore. So I told her maybe it was jet lag or I was just really exhausted from the travel, and that she should stay up as long as she wanted, but I was ready to hit the sack. Which I did. For about thirty minutes. And then it started again. I awoke with a start to what seemed even worse than the night before. I lay there contemplating waking her – but what would be the point? She would feel bad. I would feel bad. Maybe I could request to switch roommates… but what would I say? I could say I have allergies to something in the cottage, allergies to *snoring*, ha ha! Okay, Kelly was my friend, but it felt like this whole snoring thing might be kind of a deal breaker as far as rooming together. Then, after going through a number of scenarios where I would try to switch living situations, I began to imagine walking over to Kelly and putting my pillow over her head. The snoring got worse and worse.

I was clearly suffering from a wicked combination of lack of sleep, culture shock and jet lag. I then convinced myself that if interns studying to be doctors could go with no sleep during their residency, I could do this. It would be good practice for having a baby later in life, or maybe I would fall in love with a snorer and this is my training. Then, I simply admitted it – it was hell. Sleep deprivation is a form of torture. Kelly was torturing me.

Chapter Five

The first day of classes was very foggy for me to say the least. I was on night two of no sleep, so everything sort of seemed like a dream. I remember thinking one guy in my grammar class was cute, but of course I was sleep-deprived so my judgment may have been slightly off. I remember realizing my Spanish was not that bad compared to some of the other students, and felt a little boost in my confidence when one of the teachers said I spoke very well. Much of what we did was repeat our teachers. They would say something in their perfect Spanish and then we would repeat it in our imperfect Spanish until it became less and less imperfect. We read aloud a lot and this is where I shined. Even as tired as I was, I loved the challenge of reading out loud. That first day of classes felt good. This is why I came here. Luckily for me the following day was Saturday.

Thankfully the school arranged that we arrive, have orientation, one day of classes and then a weekend to recuperate. THANK GOD! I was not sure if I could go another night without sleep. Which is exactly what happened – but not because of Kelly, but because of Enrique (you remember Enrique, Elena's son). That day when Kelly and I returned from school we saw an unfamiliar car parked in Elena's driveway. As we entered the house we heard laughing, and at first sight of Enrique both Kelly and I stopped. He looked like Ricky Martin – dark featured, slender build, big smile – very handsome.

As we sat down for some juice that Alita served, Elena said that she had called Enrique to see if he might come by and meet us and then show us the town a bit that evening. She raved about how he was so successful at his work and had recently been promoted. He worked for a bank as part of upper management, mainly managing the loans operations department. His specialty was "escrow." He was very responsible and had a lot of people he oversaw on a day-to-day basis, she bragged. As she continued her praise, he sat and smiled and every now and again would try to stop his mom from making him blush, although you could tell in a way that he loved it.

His English was very good, but the subtle accent he still carried made him even more attractive. I always loved accents and found imperfect English to be quite endearing. I was hoping it was the same for the poor souls that had to listen to Kelly and I speaking our beginner Spanish, but had a feeling that was not universally the case. In fact, just that afternoon, when Kelly and I had been dropped off by the bus we took from our school each day, we swore we heard a couple local passengers laugh at us and mock us a bit as we said in our gringa accents to the other students on the bus, "Aah-dee-ohs, boo-eh-nahs no-chays!"

So, Enrique said he and a couple co-worker friends of his would come by and pick us up for dinner at around seven p.m., and maybe after we could take a tour of the city. Now, I am thinking, do I go or not? I was tired as hell and going out with a couple of 30 year olds who work in, what was it again, "loan operations" at a bank, sounded pretty dull to me, even if one of them did resemble Ricky Martin. I had hoped I would not fall asleep just listening to Elena describe what he did – imagine a bunch of his co-workers unloading on us about things like "escrow" and "loans" and "upper management this and upper management that…." Yawn already! But Kelly spoke for the both of us and said, "Perfect! Seven it is!"

So I decided to rally and said, "Yes, see you at seven!"

Kelly had brought a ton of cute dresses and made me try on a couple. I had to admit, it was fun to get dolled up and I was feeling a second wind coming on. We played music and got ready and laughed about the passengers making fun of us on the bus that day. We were quizzing each other on basic words, and when I asked her how to say "truck" in Spanish she gave me a dumbfounded look and said, "I don't know… truck-o?" I burst out laughing at the way she said it in almost a redneck kind of way, and we agreed that any word we did not know we would just add an "o" on the end of and call it a day. "Computer-o," "Dashboard-o," "Walmart-o." We just kept coming up with them and began to get a bit giddy.

Chapter Six

Before we knew it Elena was calling from the house that Enrique was there. We grabbed our purses, shut off the lamp in our perfect little cottage, and laughed as we said, "Lamp-o" and "purse-o" while walking to the house and then out to the street where Enrique's car was parked. Enrique was a perfect gentleman, holding open the car door for us. As we climbed into his car we saw that two of his friends sat in the back seat. After a bit of musical car seats, we agreed it would be best to have Kelly and I and his one friend, José, in the back and then his other friend Javier in the front.

They were all dressed in slacks, button down shirts, and ties, and the smell of a mix of several different types of colognes and hair gel filled the car. I noticed how slicked back all of their hair was; add in Kelly's perfume and my lotion and that car was a potpourri of scents that seemed to go together quite nicely. After we waved to Elena we made our awkward introductions, half in English and half in bad Spanish, and I started to notice how truly attractive Enrique and his friends were. Javier was blond with green eyes, but had the caramel skin and a smile that was up there with Ryan Gosling's. José was dark featured like Enrique but had these dark, smoldering eyes and a big smile that accented his white teeth and sexy jaw line. Now, I was not going to Mexico to meet guys, that is for sure, but I had to admit this was a nice little surprise.

Enrique explained that we were going to a little party that one of his friends was having and there would be food there. I was relieved to know we were not going to sit in some stuffy restaurant, and realized very quickly that Enrique may be very responsible at work, but after hours he may have had another personality, because all of a sudden he drew a silver flask out of his jacket pocket and passed it back, saying that on the way it was time for happy hour. His other two friends let out a hoot and holler and suddenly, before I knew it, cigarettes were being passed around the car and each of his friends brought out their flasks. As I turned to Kelly to see her reaction, I realized she had a party side to her, too, because she was taking a drink from one of the flasks and let out a loud "yeeeehaaaw!" The guys LOVED the "yeehaww" and asked what it meant, and then began repeating it over and over until everybody was laughing.

I took a drink from the flask, thinking, well, as the saying goes, "When in Rome, Roam," and turned to see Kelly lighting up a cigarette with one hand while clutching a flask in the other; well, she was a roaming, that is for sure. By the way she was trying to light her cigarette it was obvious she did not usually smoke, so José helped her. The sun had gone down by that point, and it may have been for the best because if you have never been to Mexico and have never ridden in the back seat of a car driven by a Mexican who is turning around to talk to you while flailing his cigarette around like he has all the room in the world you would want to turn off the lights and see as little as possible.

I felt like I was on a ride at Six Flags as we zoomed in and out between other cars, taxis passing us with just an inch to spare, the music blaring, and everybody shouting out "yeeeehaws!" and passing flasks and cigarettes around. I felt like I was in a moving casino for crying out loud! At one point Enrique turned around, keeping one arm on the steering wheel, and went on to request that people in the back seat be careful of their cigarette ashes because he had just had the seats reupholstered and did not want to get any cigarette burns in the new material. This request lasted about forty-five seconds because he kept getting interrupted by "yeehaws!" and the whole forty-five seconds nobody was watching the road except for me! I felt like I was having one of those bad dreams where you find yourself driving with your eyes closed and for the life of you, you cannot open them and you are just praying you will not hit an innocent pedestrian or crash into a Papa John's, and then for a second you can open them and you are amazed you are still driving and then suddenly your eyes shut and once again you are driving solely on faith. That is what that car ride felt like. It was like driving a casino on wheels… while blind.

And that was just the car ride! Once we arrived at the location of the party, I was even more astonished. I started to wonder if Enrique really worked at a bank. The house where the party was being held was immaculate – a mansion, with two outdoor pools and ponds all lit up with brightly colored koi fish in them. The trees were lit with different colored lights, and not just your crappy plastic Christmas lights from Walmart, but with big beautiful lights that created perfect lighting which shimmered off the pools and ponds giving everybody a radiant glow. There must have been about a hundred people at the party – some swimming in the pool, some sitting at tables surrounding the pool or walking around mingling. Beautiful women in their twenties to mid-thirties wandered around in cute dresses and bathing suits, mingling and dancing with equally attractive men. There was a table with plates of food and bottles of wine and beer. Enrique began introducing Kelly and me to all his friends, most of whom spoke pretty good English.

Shots of tequila were had, and I think that because I was going on such little sleep the drinks were hitting me faster than normal, so I babied them and made sure to eat and drink water in between celebratory shots. Kelly, on the other hand, seemed to have a cigarette in one hand the whole time and a drink in the other and was getting pretty chummy with José, who continued to put cigarettes in her mouth every time she would say in a slur, "Un cigarillo más, por favor" ("One more cigarette, please").

José seemed to be taking the role of Kelly's personal Spanish tutor, and I was beginning to realize that it might be my responsibility to make sure we both made it home safely that night. The problem was, I was not even sure where we were. That did not matter, though, because the party was not the last destination of the evening, and just before Kelly, cigarette in mouth, announced that she was going to jump in the pool with her clothes on, Enrique stopped her and rallied Javier, José and a couple other of his friends and announced that we were going to go to a discoteca (dance club). He explained it was "culturally essential" that Kelly and I experience a real discoteca in Mexico. It was now midnight, and I figured that I better stick with Elena's "responsible son" instead of taking any chances on calling a taxi and ending up on the wrong side of the tracks.

So once again we piled into the moving casino, which is what I called Enrique's car from then on. He laughed when I told him that, and put his arm around me and said "Es un casino que mueve." I stared back at him blankly, but also a little excited that he had put his arm around me. He said again, "Un casino que se mueve, me gusta cómo piensas, Melissa – eres muy linda" ("A casino that moves, I like how you think, Melissa – you are very cute").

Okay, I will admit, that did make me gush a bit, and I decided that maybe, just maybe, I should let loose a bit and stop trying to be so responsible because obviously I was going to have to stick with the program and genuinely roam, just like Kelly – who at that moment seemed like she was going to pass out on José's shoulder. As we approached the discoteca, all I could see was a line that wrapped around the building and kept going all the way to the parking lot.

I looked at Kelly and thought, "she will never make it." The girl could barely keep her head up as it was. But instead, Enrique pulled up to the valet and a young guy approached the car. In their fast Spanish they greeted each other with a handshake and a brief exchange, and before I knew it we were being let in a special side door. Enrique explained that the young man was a friend of the family's and that he always gave them special treatment when they showed up at the discoteca.

As we entered the club, all I could see was a sea of people dancing underneath a bunch of strobe lights. The music blared, and as I looked up I saw that the club had three levels. Enrique told me there were all sorts of different rooms – one for techno, one for rock, one for rap, salsa, even country. We decided to go to the salsa room and Enrique promised me a dance lesson. I helped José basically carry Kelly into the room. We got a table and ordered a bottle of tequila.

Because I had been pacing myself all night, I was still able to partake in the first toast, to which we all said in a loud chorus, "Yeehaaaw!"

Poor Kelly was missing it all as she basically lay face-down on the table. A couple times I tried to rouse her, and as I was close to her face I listened to see if she was snoring. Nope, of course not! Quiet as a mouse. Now I knew the trick. Get her completely hammered and then let her sleep like a baby.

Enrique pulled me out on the dance floor and said, "Es la hora para tu lección de salsa," to which I stared at him blankly. He chuckled and said loudly, "It is time for your salsa lesson."

Now I had to admit, I did not know a thing about salsa, and I felt like a dope out there as he tried to show me how to swivel my hips. After several songs I was getting it, and he was spinning me to and fro. I must say I was a GREAT spinner. I had taken figure skating lessons as a kid, and my favorite thing was to get spinning as fast as I could. I had great balance and even Enrique commented on my great spinning ability.

Then Javier asked me to dance. And he, too, commented on my spinning ability. José tried to rouse Kelly but she was out – and I mean *out!* I watched as Enrique danced with a girl who REALLY knew how to salsa – it was amazing. It was like *Dancing with the Stars* on premium gasoline – mainly because it was so real and not staged. After watching and admiring the dancing for a while I started to get a bit sleepy and wondered what time it was. I took Kelly's hand and flipped it over to look at her watch and was astonished when I saw that it was four a.m. FOUR A.M.! That blew my mind. The night had gone so quickly! I began to wonder if every weekend was like this. If so, I would not survive. Just as I was about to ask Enrique when we would be headed home, he rallied everybody and declared that it was time to go and find the perfect spot for the sunrise.

I was too tired to fight the plan, although I really just wanted to go home at that point. As we drove away from the club I put my head on Kelly's shoulder and fell asleep. The next thing I knew, I woke up and we were parked on a mountain overlooking the city below. Kelly had woken and must have gotten her second (or third) wind, because she was asking when we were going to get breakfast. I was groggy, but as soon as I got a good look at the overlook we sat upon and the sun began to make its ascension above the city below my third wind kicked in as well, and I felt an immense appreciation for the previous night's adventure. Here I was, sitting on a mountaintop watching the sun come up in Mexico after having danced all night.

As we sat there, Javier pulled out a clay bottle and started to pull the cork out of it. I noticed it was just a plain jug with no label on it.

"Yeeehaw! The pulque!" shouted José.

"What is pulque?" Kelly asked, indicating she wanted José to pass her the bottle. "Pasalo por favor" ("Pass it to me"), she demanded.

"Ooooohhh, look who learned a new phrase in Spanish thanks to her tutor," chided José. José handed her the bottle of pulque and she tossed back her head and took a big drink.

The expression on her face indicated that maybe it was one of those drinks that you should actually sip, like brandy. Her nose crinkled and she gasped.

"¡Dulce! ¡ES DULCE!" she gurgled, coughing as her eyes watered. "Sweet! IT'S SWEET!" she exclaimed.

"Pulque is an indigenous beverage," said Enrique. "It is made from the agave plant."

He then took the bottle and took a small drink. "It is not known who actually invented pulque, but it goes back at least a thousand years. Various stories and myths have developed as to its origins. Most involve Mayahuel, the goddess of the maguey plant. It was thought that the aguamiel collecting in the center of the plant was her blood." We used our pocket translator to look up "maguey" and learned it means "aloe." We then looked up "aguamiel" and learned it means "honey water."

"I am not sure what the truth is, but our indigenous ancestors drank it. It is very sacred," Enrique said.

"And it will get you drunk as a skunk if you are not careful!" exclaimed Javier, who then proceeded to take a drink the size that Kelly had taken.

As the sun rose above the horizon, Enrique rallied everybody once more and we made our final trip back to our little casita, finishing the pulque on the way. At the cottage we said our "hasta luegos" and promised we would do it again soon. After entering our room both Kelly and I fell into our little beds and passed out until two o'clock that afternoon. I am not sure if Kelly snored or not because I was out like a log and it felt like the best sleep I had ever had.

Chapter Seven

We woke to Elena calling us for lunch, and sure enough, when Alita put down our plates there was chicken on all of them. Kelly, hung over and a little weak simply said, "gracias," and proceeded to eat everything but the chicken.

"If you squeeze some lime on it, it is amazing," I said to her with a smirk, and she gave me a look as if to say, "Shut the hell up."

After our late lunch we went back to our casita and both took some time to organize our materials for the following day. We quizzed each other a bit more on words, took showers, and got our laundry bags ready for the next day. That was another awesome perk about this program. Each Monday students would bring their dirty clothes to the school where they would be laundered, and then the students would pick them up at the end of the day and bring them home. This way the host families would not bear the economic burden and wear and tear on their washing machines.

Later we ate a small dinner with Elena. Alita had Sundays off, so we ordered pizza from a local place that Elena liked, plain cheese for Kelly and a Supreme for Elena and me.

While eating we watched one of Alita's favorite telanovelas. We were told that watching television was a great way to practice our Spanish, so not to feel bad about spending time watching programs no matter how cheesy and overly melodramatic they were. These telanovelas make *Days of Our Lives* seem like an after-school special if you ask me! It is like if you compare the way white people dance to the way Latinos dance – white people square dance, Latinos practically have sex on the dance floor – that is the difference. So we watched, me trying to hold in laughter as I imagined each of the over dramatized scenes as a spoof on *Saturday Night Live* (much like the current skit, "The Californians"), and Elena and Kelly (who apparently had become a smoker now) sat there sharing a cigarette and watching intently as Roberto accused Natalia of poisoning his mother or as Milagros wept at the funeral of her daughter who died in a fatal car accident that was under investigation as a pre-meditated homicide.

After almost two hours of telenovelas I was not sure if my Spanish had improved, but I was certainly tired and ready for bed. I said goodnight to Elena and Kelly. Kelly said she was going to finish watching the program because she wanted to know if Soledad was really pregnant or just faking it in order to get Reynaldo to marry her, and so we bid our good nights and I hoped and prayed that Kelly would not snore that night as I slipped into my little bed smelling the sweet scent of flowers wafting into our room.

As I lay there I chuckled to myself about the fact that neither Enrique nor José nor Javier mentioned work even once the whole time we were together, and the more time I spent abroad the more I began to realize how work obsessed North Americans are and how there is so much more to life than punching a clock – like dancing salsa, seeing the sun rise from a special place, and saying cheers (or Yeeeehaaaw!) to new friends while sharing a sacred drink. I also realized that Kelly had broken out of her box a bit by accepting the fact that she may just have to eat food that was cooked with chicken every now and again because Alita was not going to back down on the issue. And I broke out of my shell by realizing that I may have to room with someone who snores.

I was already learning how to deal with some of the more subtle rules of life… which ones do we abide by, which do we break, and which do we work to change.

Chapter Eight

So after drifting to sleep feeling positive about the opportunities to grow more as a person I was experiencing, I awoke to Kelly entering the room and whispering she was sorry and would be very quiet. She and Elena had stayed up and watched one more program. Well, Kelly was quiet getting ready for bed, but the minute her head hit the pillow it began. The snoring started. This time it was a whistle that grew louder and louder and then would stop and then start again. I could not believe it! Before we left for Mexico everybody warned us about getting roofied (you know, the rape drug). I wished I could have scored myself some at the club the other night, because if I had some I would have crushed it up into her piece of damn cheese pizza and would not have felt a bit sorry about it.

How unfair was this?! At that moment I decided I would never marry a man who snored. Sleep is way more precious than love, I decided. At one point I coughed really loud to wake her, hoping she would fall back asleep and not snore, but nope, she just grunted a little, rolled over and began to snore a snore that I decided to name the Cement Truck snore. For heaven's sake, I was now naming her snores!

There was the Andy Griffith snore – that was the one where she whistles. Then there was the Ha! I Faked You Out Again snore – the one where she would be quiet for a minute, just long enough to make you think she was done, and then start up again. And lastly, there was the Delores Claiborne snore, the one that made you feel like you could actually murder someone in their sleep with the very pillow they rested their damn snoring heads on. OMG, how is it possible that a girl who weighed no more than 120 pounds like Kelly could snore so loudly!?!?!?! I looked over at her as she lay there. That sweet, freckled face did not match the sounds coming out of her.

At that moment I began wondering if God was punishing me for something. Was it the tattoo I got when I turned eighteen? Was getting a tattoo a sin? Is ninety-percent of Los Angeles inhabited by sinners? Because ninety percent of Los Angelinos have tattoos I am pretty sure. Should the City of Angels really be called the City of Sinners, which in Spanish would be "Los Pecadores." "Los Angeles" sounded so much better than "Los Pecadores," in my opinion.

Of course, Los Angeles is pretty much run by Jewish people, everybody knows that. But I like Jewish people. Jerry Seinfeld… come on! Jerry is a good person. Who doesn't like Jerry Seinfeld? Or Barbara Streisand? Who doesn't like Babs? Okay, okay… I guess I could think of a couple people that may think Barbara Streisand is annoying. Okay, okay. Lack of sleep was making me think like a person high on dope. Which made me wish I had some. I would slip some of that into Kelly's food. Make her a big ol' vegetarian "pot" pie – knock her right out.

What was God trying to teach me, I pondered? Maybe he was teaching me that sometimes you have to just be honest with someone and be assertive. Or was he telling me to be patient? I just felt that telling Kelly would make her feel bad, and I knew she could not help her snoring. It was a damn curse for crying out loud. Then I realized the question I should have been asking is, "What on earth is God punishing Kelly for?" I mean, anyone who snores like that must have done something *reaallly* awful.

Had Kelly killed a person? She did have that other personality – the party side I hadn't known about. Maybe she had multiple personalities and one of them killed someone and snoring was her punishment. I mean, all of a sudden she is a smoker? Really? What else was she hiding? I knew Kelly was Irish – so maybe she was Catholic and all it would take would be to go to confession and do about 98,000 Hail Mary's and she would be rid of this blasted snoring curse God had bestowed upon her. I decided one of the first things I needed to do the following day would be to ask if she was Catholic and go from there.

So as to not go completely crazy just laying there, I decided to open the travel journal my mom had bought for me and I started to write a bit. I decided that the following day I would take a nap immediately after I got home and would just bear through the night. I wrote for an hour about everything, including Kelly's snoring, and my theories on why we were both suffering from this horrific curse, and our night out with Enrique, my classes, the telanovelas, etcetera. And then, at about 1:30 a.m. when I could not write anymore, I had the brilliant idea of sneaking into the main house with my blanket and sleeping on the couch. But I did not have a key.

So I imagined ways of getting a key. I could roofie Elena one night, take her keys, get a copy made and then…

nooooo… that was not going to work. I could just imagine her not waking up and suddenly my face would be all over the papers, the headlines would read, "American Student Charged with Roofie-ing Mexican Host Mother." The media would eat that one up for sure. No, no. I had to come up with a better plan than roofie-ing Elena.

Ugghhhhh….

Then I decided that maybe I could somehow reposition Kelly, turn her on her side, wrap duct tape around her mouth… okay, okay, that was not nice – plus, I did not have any duct tape. So maybe I could just start with repositioning Kelly on her side. Sometimes that helps. So I've heard. From friends whose fathers snore. I did not even think females could snore, to be honest. It is always someone's dad who snores, and generally he would be some burly-looking dude with a hairy back and a mustache and beard, not some petite, strawberry-blonde haired, blue-eyed college girl.

So I slowly walked to her bed and very quickly nudged her onto her side and then in one swift move jumped back into my bed and lay down. She grunted, let out a moan, and then God, the angels and the pecadores must have stepped in because she FINALLY shut up long enough for me to fall asleep. I woke up the next morning grateful to have had four solid hours of sleep that night.

Chapter Nine

The next day was Monday – time for our very first Monday in Mexico. I was groggy, but still grateful for the little sleep I had managed to get. After our breakfast, Kelly and I gathered our book bags and laundry bags and made our way to the bus stop. We had not been on a Monday morning bus before this, and when it arrived it was definitely more packed than the other days we had taken it; so packed, in fact, that we had to stand – which was no big deal – but as the bus stopped and more people crammed on we found ourselves wedged between some pretty strong-smelling men, our laundry bags each taking up extra space and making it that much more awkward.

I wedged my laundry bag between my head and the window and ended up falling asleep for ten minutes. Kelly woke me, laughing at the fact that I had fallen asleep while standing up on the bus. "Wake up, sleepy McGee!" she said, poking me in the ribs. I awoke with a start and so wished I had the nerve to tell her why I was so tired, but I merely chuckled and said I maybe needed one more cup of coffee that morning.

"You know too much caffeine is not good for you?" she said, poking me again.

"Yeah, well, getting roofied isn't either," I wanted to say, but chose to ignore it and instead said, "I wonder how you say "duct tape" in Spanish."

"What?" she chuckled. "Why?"

"Just curious," I said, smiling to myself. As we walked the six blocks from where the bus dropped us off to the school, I asked Kelly if she happened to be Catholic.

"Well, I was baptized, but we never really went to church growing up," she answered (like about eighty percent of Catholics I know). "Why do you ask?"

"Just curious…" I said, reveling in the thought that she still could be saved. She just may have to say more Hail Mary's than I had originally calculated.

"You are sure curious about some random things, Chica!" she said, skipping a bit as we crossed the intersection.

"Yep, I sure am!" I replied.

Despite my being really tired, classes went well for the most part that day. In my grammar class I sat looking around, wondering if anyone else was paired up with a snorer. Or was I the only one? Everyone looked pretty well rested to me. During one of my basic reading and vocabulary classes, one student had trouble pronouncing a word which caused a break out of chuckles in the classroom that made me feel like I was back in elementary school laughing while some class clown played a practical joke on another student – one like dumping pencil sharpener shavings on another student's head, for example. Or one of my favorite stories my mom would tell about how when she was a kid in Catholic school, being taught solely by nuns, every now and again some precocious student would scrape their rubber-soled shoe across the floor to make it sound like a loud fart and all the students would bust out laughing, leaving the poor nun clueless as to who did it. Then the ruler would come out and the class would quiet down until the next practical joke was played. Well, this situation was a bit different because the student was not trying to make the class laugh, which I guess made it funnier, but it was still one of those things that was impossible to not laugh at.

We were learning new words and repeating them out loud. The word at hand was "enfocar," which in English means, "to focus." One of the students in my class was asked to read it out loud. If said with a horrible accent, which this particular student had and could not seem to get over, the word sounded much like "En-FOCK-ar." Now this is pre-*Meet the Fockers*, but you catch the drift. I am not sure why it is, but no matter what, when someone repeats over and over a word that resembles the "F" word, it is funny.

For example, my other nephew (Jesse's younger brother, Jake) had a hard time pronouncing his 't's for a bit. He would pronounce them with an 'f' sound instead. One day we were all riding in the car and a big rig passed us. In the most enthusiastic, loud voice he could muster, my sweet little nephew exclaimed, "BIG FRUCK! BIG FRUCK!" while pointing at the truck. Needless to say, all the adults in the car had a hard time holding in their laughter as he kept repeating it over and over, "LOOK AT THE BIG FRUCK!" Finally, because my stomach hurt so bad from trying not to laugh too loud, I requested that my brother pass the damn thing already before we all burst into hysterics.

So, in a similar fashion, the poor kid in my Spanish class just could not grasp the word and kept repeating, "En-FOCK-ar." The first time he said it only a couple people laughed. I did not laugh because I figured he would get it right the next time since everybody makes a mistake now and again.

After the teacher corrected him and he once again repeated "en-fock-ar," a couple more people laughed. It was obvious he was not aware of the mistake he was making because there was no smirk on his face; in fact, he looked completely frustrated, and once again when he was corrected by the teacher he looked up and asked, "I said that, didn't I?"

The teacher, in Spanish, said, "No, tu dijiste, 'en-FOCK-ar' y la pronunciación corecta es, 'en- FOE- car', no 'en-FOCK-ar'" ("No, you said 'en-FOCK-ar' and the correct pronunciation is 'en-FOE-car,' not 'en-FOCK-ar'"). She then had him break down the word into parts so he was saying very loudly, "FOKE" and "FOCK." By this time the whole class was shaking in unison, trying not to bust out in laughter.

"Veas la diferencia?" ("Do you see the difference?"), the professor asked the student, taking her glasses off and wiping them on her blouse, repeating "FOKE, no FOCK," as she put her newly shined-up glasses back on, seemingly completely unaware of what was so funny. So now, with the professor saying the "F" word over and the student repeating her with a confused look on his face, the whole class felt like we were watching a profanity laden Mexican version of the classic "Who's on First?" skit.

I made it through the day with a little more energy than I expected, and by the time Kelly and I were ready to head home I was in good spirits. Kelly and I laughed the whole way home on the bus as I told her about the whole "enfocar" incident, and we agreed that at least our accents were not that bad. After we got home, Kelly went to visit with Elena for a bit and smoke some cigarettes with her while I took a nice two hour long nap that seemed to replenish me enough to wake up for some dinner. Alita made a pasta that actually did not have meat in it, and over dinner Elena told us about how she met her late husband Enrique and how he was the only man she had ever been with and did not think she would meet anybody else.

Chapter Ten

Elena told us she met Enrique Sr. when she was applying for college. He was working in the cafeteria of the college as a cook during the day while taking night classes to become an engineer, and he had seen her sitting at a table filling out an application for the college. He was only a couple of years older than she was, but had a very mature look to him, and when he put on a hat, tie and glasses it was like when Clark Kent goes into a phone booth and comes back out – whole different person.

So after spotting Elena from across the cafeteria, Enrique Sr. went to his locker, changed into his slacks and white button down shirt, borrowed a hat from one friend and a tie from another, took the glasses right off another friend's face, then walked straight up to Elena and told her he was a professor at the school and if she needed any help to call him and gave her his number. He said he liked to greet new applicants and make sure they had all their questions answered. She gave him her information, thinking it would be good in case she had any questions. He knew at that moment he was going to somehow marry that dark-eyed beauty he saw from across the room. It was love at first sight, he told all his buddies.

Now to some people this may seem shady or down-right wrong, but he felt it was his only way of not letting the woman he knew he was destined to be with walk right out of the door as he stood there frying papas fritas (french fries). So he called her that night to see how the application was going, and said that he could offer some advice on the essay part if she wanted to meet for coffee the next day – to which Elena agreed. They met at a café near the college, and he showed up with a bouquet of flowers for her. The minute she sat down, perplexed as to why a professor would bring her a bouquet of flowers, he told her the truth. He said he had seen her and all he could think of was to pretend he was a professor in order to talk to her, and that he understood if she got up and walked away at that moment, but that he would appreciate five minutes of her time and if, after five minutes, she was uninterested he would never bother her again – and they never parted from that day.

He did, in fact, help her write her entrance application essay that day while they sat in that little café, and she did get into the design program she applied to, but two years into it little Enriquito was born and she became a full-time mother. After having Enriquito she was told she could not have any more children, so she dedicated her time and energy to being the best mother and wife she could be. She said she and Enrique Sr. grew more and more in love as the years went by, unlike some of her friends whose marriages fell apart, and she missed him every day.

After Elena related her story, Kelly and I sat, both going on and on about how it was like a scene from a movie and how romantic and wasn't she scared he was a total wacko and she said, "When you know, you know. Love is kinda crazy."

Alita brought out some chocolate caliente (hot chocolate) and Elena brought out a picture album and showed us pictures from their wedding day. Another story that made us almost cry.

Neither Elena nor Enrique Sr. came from wealthy families; in fact they were both quite poor. So for their wedding they had a very small ceremony in the back yard of Elena's parents' home and then, for their honeymoon, she, dressed in her white wedding dress, and he, in his suit, got on a city bus and took it twelve hours to the ocean. Everybody on the bus clapped for them, and as they got off the bus a newspaper reporter covering a story about the plight of the fishermen in the little town in which they were spending their honeymoon took a picture of them. The next day the photo made the front page of the town's newspaper.

The headline read, "A Pesar de los Tiempos Duros, el Amor Siempre Gana" ("Despite Hard Times, Love Always Wins"). Elena showed us the original clipping from the newspaper, and we just sat and swooned at the story as she put away the album. She finished by saying she had always wanted to go back to the city in which she and her husband had spent their honeymoon, but it was too hard without her Enrique.

She then invited us to watch her all time favorite telanovela, *Al Diablo con los Guapos* (*Down with the Beautiful*). And as tempting as it was to see a show called *Down with the Beautiful*, I said thanks but I was going to take a shower, write in my journal a bit, and then hit the sack. Kelly jumped on the offer and asked if she could change into her pajamas and get comfy. Elena said yes, and Kelly and I walked back to our casita gushing about Elena's story.

I was happy that Kelly liked those telanovelas and that Elena now had someone to spend time with in the evenings.

Elena seemed lonely, and I thought maybe that was part of the reason she allowed exchange students stay with her. Kelly said she would be in later and would try to be as quiet as possible – to which I thanked her while trying not to say something like, "Could ya maybe drink a bottle of vodka with Elena while watching *Down With the Beautiful* and just pass out on the lawn on your way back?" But I bit my tongue and told her to have fun.

Well, once again God must have been on my side, because that night Kelly actually fell asleep on the couch in the main house. She came in at six the next morning and said she had fallen asleep watching the telanovela, so Elena just put a blanket on her and let her sleep in the living room on the couch. "Hallelujah!" was my first thought. My next thought at that point was, did Elena get any sleep that night? Were the walls thick enough in the house to muffle the Andy Griffith or the Delores Claiborne? Maybe Enrique was a snorer too, and Elena was used to the Cement Truck. Nonetheless, God bless the telanovela *Al Diablo con los Guapos*, because that was the first night I had slept a full eight hours since we had arrived a week prior.

When we went to sit down for breakfast, Elena joined us. I could not tell if she looked more tired than normal, but I did inquire how many nights a week *Al Diablo con los Guapos* was on. Damn, just Monday evenings. Well, hopefully this staying on the couch becomes a Monday thing, and then a Tuesday thing and then a Wednesday thing and so forth. To have my own little cottage in Mexico for the next couple months would be a dream come true!

Chapter Eleven

Each Tuesday the school planned for a one-day excursion to Mexico City, which is located about a half an hour from Cuernavaca, so that students had a chance to see some of the most historic sights of the city. The first Tuesday the school planned to visit the main plaza in Mexico City, "The Plaza de la Constitución," or what is commonly known as "the Zocalo." Our excursion leader explained that the Zocalo is the main square of Mexico City's historic center. He said it's one of the largest public squares in the world. In the center one cannot miss the towering Mexican flag hovering over the plaza. "This is the heart of the city where many events, festivals, concerts and protests take place," he explained.

It definitely was a hub of action and people. As you looked around, you would see a mix of tourists, locals and vendors co-mingling as the huge Mexican flag waved overhead. Our guide explained that Zocalo means "pedestal" or "stand," and that in the 1800s a pedestal was set up in the center of the square for a monument to commemorate Mexican independence. The planned statue was never put in place, and people began to refer to the square itself as the Zocalo. Now in many towns in Mexico the main square is called the Zocalo.

After the short tour we were to have lunch there and then an hour of free time to wander about, buy some souvenirs, explore the plaza, and then get back on the bus to head home. The tour was fascinating despite the fact that it felt like we were being herded around like cattle, but what are you gonna do? As we completed the tour we ended up at the southeast corner of the Zocolo, where we learned that Mexico City is actually built on top of the Aztec capital, Tenochtitlan, and at that moment we were standing on the very spot where Hernán Cortés is said to have met Montezuma, the Aztec emperor, in 1519.

"After the Spaniards conquered the Aztecs," our guide explained, "Cortés had the colonial town plan drawn according to Spanish tradition, with the square in the middle of the city, surrounded by buildings which symbolize the colonial powers: the church and the government." I sat and thought about that for a moment. In high school we studied a bit of world history, but it was not until standing in that plaza that it sunk in. These were real events that had actually happened, and I was standing on the very ground on which they took place. It was not until years later that I began to understand about the conquest of the Aztecs and how I actually felt about it. I was then just touching the surface as I looked down at my feet and thought about the other feet that had stood there before me. Not only was my bubble being broken, my perspective was changing because I was gaining more of it. This was only to intensify the more I got out of my bubble and the more I traveled. I started to realize that many of the textbooks we study in school in the United States come from only one point of view as opposed to representing all sides of the equation.

The tour guide continued to tell more facts throughout lunch, but to be honest with you, one of the most impactful things I can actually remember from that day was something that happened during our free hour. Kelly and I were sitting on a bench, mainly people-watching, and out of nowhere a little girl with long dark hair, about ten years old, approached us and asked for some money. She spoke a little English. She was dressed in a plaid skirt and a white shirt, which made me think she went to school. We gave her a little money, which was a no-no according to our school policy, but no one was watching so we did it anyway.

All of a sudden a couple other little girls came up dressed the same, ranging from seven to twelve years old. We gave them all the rest of the money we had and showed them that we had no more money by letting them look in our purses and pockets. They were fascinated by the things we had in our purses, like the little mirror I had and Kelly's camera. We began talking with them and I asked if they went to school. The very first girl that approached us said they did not, but nonetheless she was going to be a famous surgeon some day. She then began to inspect my leg using my mirror as what she described as her magnifying glass and pretended to perform surgery on my leg. Then she did the same with Kelly.

She was such a little firecracker. I wondered where her parents were. Did she have parents? I asked her what her name was and she said, "Yesenia."

I then asked where her mom and dad were. She said she did not have a mom or dad, but she had una Señora. She explained that la Señora took care of her and the other girls, and that each day the girls would bring all the money they had collected that day from begging and give it to her and in exchange La Señora would care for them.

She then said quietly, though, as she plucked away at my leg, pretending to sew a stitch, that La Señora was not always very nice. She explained that was why, some day, she planned to become a famous surgeon, so she did not have to live with La Señora forever. My heart sank as I thought about the reality that these little girls lived in, and I promised myself to never complain about Kelly's snoring again.

At least I had a bed and a roof over my head and the opportunities to study and be healthy. I wished I could have taken all those little girls home with me to Minnesota, although they may have hated me for it after one freezing winter, and would likely have pleaded for me to take them back to their Señora, but that really was the first time I saw poverty at that level. I wanted to give Yesenia my mirror because she was so in love with it, but I did not want the other girls to feel left out. This was a toughie. I then said that I believed one day she would be a famous surgeon. She then handed me the mirror and said, 'Yo sé! Un dia voy a ser una doctora famosa, ustedes verán!" ("I know! One day I will be a famous doctor – you will all see!")

At that point our field trip leader came over and said the bus was loading. We said goodbye to the little girls, and as we walked away we saw them approach another small group of what looked like tourists and ask them for money. The whole bus ride back I felt this heaviness in my heart. Why were some people born into poverty while others into riches? Since that day, this has been one of the questions that truly does keep me up at night. Why this disparity? That night I went to bed with one thought on my mind. What was I going to do in my life to help kids like Yesenia? How could I use my life to improve the lives of those like Yesenia? That day at the plaza was a true eye-opener for me and definitely took me out of my box. Yes, Kelly snored that night, and yes, I did keep complaining in my head about it, but my thoughts continued to be with the little girls in the plaza. I finally fell asleep around three in the morning after having written in my journal for about an hour about the day's happenings.

The next few days were very busy with school projects and homework. Classes were going well and I found my Spanish to be improving more and more as the days went by. I took naps after school while Kelly went inside the house and chatted with Elena as they watched their afternoon telanovelas. Already I was becoming aware of how quickly the time was flying. Before we knew it another weekend was upon us.

Chapter Twelve

The school had arranged that one Saturday a month students would have a chance to go on an excursion if they wanted to get more involved in community service. The school chose the organization and we had the chance to participate as much as we could. Immediately I checked "yes" on the form and indicated I wanted to go on the very first excursion. I was delighted to find out that the chosen organization was actually a local orphanage. I could not believe it. After the transformative experience I had at the plaza, it seemed like God was stepping in and providing this chance for me to be around kids again. Maybe it was a sign, I thought. Maybe I would end up working at an orphanage! Hell, maybe I would end up working at this very orphanage. God works in mysterious ways, I did know that.

Kelly did not want to go, and in confidence that day, after I pressed her a bit as to why, she told me that one time she had to volunteer at a homeless shelter for a freshman college class she had taken that required students do some kind of community service. She explained that for her service she spent one night basically staying up all night at this shelter in Chicago, where she was from, with several staff members and a couple other volunteers. At first she said she felt great about it, but then as the night went on she began to get sleepy and kept nodding off.

It was the duty of the volunteers and the staff in charge to stay awake throughout the night in case of an emergency, and to watch over the guests at the shelter. After Kelly nodded off for the fourth or fifth time, one of the other regular volunteers told her a good way to stay awake and make the time pass quickly was to count the number of farts she heard throughout the night. He explained that he had to do it all the time or he would fall asleep. At first she was completely dismayed by the suggestion and thought the guy was an a-hole for suggesting it, but then, at about two in the morning, she realized it was either count the farts or fall asleep. So she began counting, and by 5:30 a.m. she counted twenty-eight audible farts. She said she left feeling so bad that she just dropped the class all together, and she wondered why the shelter did not allow for shorter shifts during the night so that staff and volunteers did not have to resort to counting farts all night to stay up.

Now, I found the story to be completely hysterical, and I thought that it was a little silly of her to totally avoid community service because of that one experience. She, on the other hand, said it sounded funny but was actually quite traumatizing. "Have you ever had to sit in a room that smelled like twenty-eight farts?" she asked me. "And that's not counting the silent bombs that usually stink the most!" she added for effect.

She wished me luck at the orphanage the next day, and told me that Elena said Enrique had called and wanted to know if we were up for going out with him and his friends again tonight. Kelly had agreed to go, but I said no because I wanted to be thoroughly rested for the following day's outing to the orphanage. As I waved Kelly, Enrique, José and Javier off that night, I felt a wave come over me. I was doing the right thing. The previous weekend had been a blast, but I did not want to risk feeling hung over and tired the following morning. I was meant for something great in life, and I had a feeling this was a door I needed to walk through.

That night I slept like a baby and awoke at six a.m. just as Kelly stumbled home, smelling like tequila and cigarettes and telling me what a great time I had missed and how she had the funniest story she would tell me when I got home. As she hit her pillow, I was out the door headed to the bus stop.

I got on the bus with about twenty other students and a couple of teachers and program staff. The orphanage, run by a priest and ten or so alumni of the orphanage, was a two-hour ride from Cuernavaca. Originally from the United States, the priest had visited Mexico many years before and, after seeing all the poverty and need for a safe place for children to live, decided to start the orphanage with the help of some nearby churches.

The orphanage was set on three acres of land and was a self-sustaining community – meaning that all the food the orphans and staff ate was actually grown on the property. The kids learned how to compost, plant and grow the crops, how to milk the cows, even how to slaughter pigs. They had classes in sewing, mechanics, pottery, carpentry, cooking, typing, reading and all the other basic academic and skill-oriented classes needed to make it in the world. There were about one hundred orphans all together, and once they turned eighteen they had the choice to either go out into the real world and find work, go to college with the help of a number of government and community based organizations, or stay on to help run the orphanage (which, we were told, about ten to fifteen a year choose to do).

The priest explained that there generally was always enough staff and the kids all had daily chores that helped in the upkeep of the orphanage. It was INCREDIBLE to say the least. We toured the orphanage and met with the staff, and then we were going to have time to spend playing with the kids. That was the part I was especially looking forward to, especially after my encounter with Yesenia and the girls in the plaza. We ate a lunch that the kids prepared and served. It was beans and rice, bread, a small salad and fresh guava juice.

One of the kitchen staff said that this was the daily meal, and on Sundays they would eat something more substantial like pork or beef. I could not believe how well-run the operations of the place were. What a brilliant idea. I already wanted to inquire how one would apply to work at the orphanage. I decided at that point that my destiny had been laid out for me. What would my mom think, I wondered? And my friends and family back home? Maybe I could just have my mom send me my things and, like Mother Teresa, I would just start working right away.

At that point I could not believe that just a week prior I was hung-over and sleeping my Saturday away while this Saturday things were so clear in my head about what I wanted to do with my life. It was almost time to go and play with the kids. I could not wait to see their sweet faces. We were told that there were about fifty of them waiting for us. As we made our way to the gymnasium-style building where they were waiting we walked by an area that was gated off. I could see kids playing behind the gate and I inquired why they were behind there. The priest stopped us and several of the kids came up to the fence.

"Well, there was a recent outbreak of chicken pox at the orphanage this past month and so we have to quarantine these poor little souls until they get better." When he said "chicken pox" I froze. "We think we have all of them here, but you know how the pox can be," the priest said as he rustled the hair of one of the little kids who stood behind the fence – his little face peering over to see us.

"Damn!" I thought. "I've never had the chicken pox." It was the one childhood malady I never had, and I had read that if you have never had them and contract them as an adult it can be really serious – even life-threatening.

Here is the kicker. I remember my mom warning me when I declared elementary education as my major to be careful of the chicken pox because I had never had them. Now here I was at a fricking orphanage in Mexico where there had been an outbreak of the damn things and the priest just said he THINKS they got all of the kids with pox behind the fence. He THINKS… or he *KNOWS?*

"You can say hello to them if you want. Lord knows they need love the most," he said with a look of genuine concern in his eyes. As I began to back away, several of the other students in my group approached the fence and started telling stories to the kids about how they had had chicken pox when they were little and not to worry, they would go away soon. One little kid with dark eyes and scruffy hair began to scratch his face, and I swear at that very moment I began to itch all over and my mind raced to the fact that I had just eaten lunch that was prepared by the kids.

What if one of the kids who helped prepare lunch had the chicken pox? My throat felt like it was beginning to close and all I could think of at that point was how fast I wanted to get away from that sick-ridden orphanage and how could I have been so stupid to come here in the first place!? Then I thought, "The person I should be angry at is this stupid priest! Why did he not warn us beforehand that there had been a breakout of the chicken pox – BEFORE A BUS LOAD OF DO-GOODER WANNABES SHOWED UP AT THE DAMN ORPHANAGE?" Would that not have been something to put out on the radar? I mean, who does this priest think I am, Mother Teresa for crying out loud?"

Keeping my inner rage to myself, I quietly approached the leader of our group and told her that I had never had the chicken pox. She took me aside and said that she would walk me to the bus, and that I should wait there for them. She asked why I had not said anything earlier and I wanted to smack her over the head with the bag of gifts I had brought for the little kids; that is, the little kids I apparently would not be playing with.

"I just did tell you! As soon as I found out there was an outbreak of chicken pox I told you!" I said, feeling like I was dealing with a bunch of morons at this point.

"Well," she said, "we will be out in about an hour. You did not touch any of the kids, did you?"

"No, but I ate food their hands touched."

"I think you will be okay," she replied. "Here is some hand sanitizer, use this."

Once again I was thinking, "*Morons!*" This woman thinks I will be okay. Is she a doctor? No! At that moment it occurred to me that I was not sure I would even want to *see* a doctor in Mexico if the people here were this irresponsible.

I tried to think back to the orientation we had and what they said about the dangers of getting medical treatment in Mexico. As I sat "quarantined" on the stupid bus with my hand sanitizer, the bag of gifts, and my fanny pack trying to figure out if I was genuinely itching or just *waaaaay* paranoid, my mind racing about the what-ifs of really having chicken pox as an adult in Mexico, a small group of kids walked past the bus and started waving and saying, "Hola mujer bonita!" ("Hello beautiful lady!")

I waved back, and they stood there for a moment. One of them picked up a reed from the ground and with nimble fingers began braiding it really quickly into the shape of a flower. It truly was amazing, and had I not been the mess of a worry that I was I would have been fawning all over them, but in my mind they all had the chicken pox, so I just sat there, mortified.

The little boy who made the flower walked to the door of the bus and began to climb the stairs. When I realized he was coming at me I tried in my best Spanish to tell him that I could not play with the kids at the orphanage because of the chicken pox. Damn it! I was racking my brain – how do you say, "Stay away, child!" in Spanish??

"Hablas inglés?" I asked at this point, backing away from the kid. Had anybody seen this they would have thought I was the meanest b-word in the world. With his big, dark eyes he smiled and shook his head no. "Damn!" I thought again. He was literally backing me into the back of the bus. Honestly… could this really be happening?

So I tried to gesture for him to stay away and just put the flower on a seat, but he just kept coming at me. By then the group of kids he was with were all gathered at the front of the bus watching the curious scenario. So I did the only thing I could think of and opened the emergency door in the back of the bus (I had always fantasized about doing that in middle school, so this was something to knock off the bucket list at least…) and jumped out. Of course the little boy followed suit.

But the jump was too high for him, so of course, like any little adorable kid would do, he reached out his sweet little arms for me to grab him. He laughed and clapped and at this point I realized he thought we were playing a game. "Damn!" I thought again. The little group of kids made their way down the stairs of the bus and came around to the back to see what we were doing. At that point I took the gifts from my bag and set them down on the ground. The kids ran up and began rifling through them. Then I took some money out of my fanny pack and, in a panic as one came at me to give me a hug, I threw the money on the ground for them. They all clamored around the money, scrambling to pick it up. I felt like there must be a hidden camera somewhere and this was all just a big joke.

The little boy was still waving at me to come and get him from the back of the bus, and when I just stood there gesturing for him to go back through the bus and come over he took a wrong step and accidentally fell out, landing on his knee. He started crying. I stood there, partly relieved that he could no longer come at me, partly hoping I would not have to pick him up and carry him anywhere, and partly still angry at that damn priest for being so saintly and stupid at the same time.

One of the staff at the orphanage had just come out of one of the huts and, seeing the commotion, ran over. He looked totally confused when he saw that I was just standing there not helping the poor crying kid. As he bent down to see if the little boy was okay I tried to explain to him that I was told to stay away from the kids because of the chicken pox and how I had never had them, to which he replied as he looked up at me, "These are not kids from the orphanage. They live over there." He pointed to an area of trees across the way.

"They sometimes come here for a little handout every now and again, but they probably don't have the chicken pox."

Again, my mind went to the key word "probably." I told him it would ease my mind to stay away from all the kids because… and went on some long-winded explanation about how I was not sure if my travel insurance covered the chicken pox and that I was somewhat leery about medical care in Mexico as it was. He just gave me a look like I was the biggest a-hole in the world and lifted the boy up. Then he and the little group walked away, giving me awkward backward glances.

At that moment I wanted to cry, and as I got back on the bus and went to shut the door I saw laying on the ground the little rose made out of reed. Had I been more like Mother Teresa, I would have picked it up and brought it home as a reminder of what I should do with my life, but alas, I was not, am not, and will never be Mother Teresa. Mother Teresa would not have been afraid of the chicken pox like I was. The bus ride home seemed to take four hours instead of two. I pretended to be asleep. A number of other students had their eyes closed or headphones on. My mind was reeling about this whole chicken pox thing. I did my best not to scratch anywhere because, one, I knew if I had contracted them scratching would only make it worse, and two, I did not want to draw any more attention to myself than I already had.

Nobody from the school saw the incident with the little kids on the bus, thank God, but several of the other students did ask why I did not play with the orphans, and I had to explain to about five different people that I had never had chicken pox and felt more comfortable staying away. Each of them had the same response. "*Ooooohhh*, I have heard that it is *reeeeaaaallly* bad to get the chicken pox as an adult! You could die from them, I heard."

To which I responded with a slight sarcastic undertone, "Yes, I know, that is why I stayed away." I was so crabby about the whole thing that in my mind all I could think was, "Morons… the whole lot of them!"

Chapter Thirteen

I was not looking forward to telling Kelly about the whole damn incident either, but sure enough, when I got back she was in our little casita waiting with bells on to hear about my day at the orphanage. She had a smirk on her face that made me think someone had already filled her in, but to my total surprise she pulled me close and whispered, "Wait, before you tell me anything, we need to smoke this!" She opened her hand and I looked down to see she was holding a joint. "I have been waiting all day to share this with you!" she giggled.

Now the last time I had tried marijuana was in high school. I had only experimented with it a handful of times, mainly to appease a couple girlfriends of mine who would not shut up about how awesome it was. To tell ya the truth, the only thing it did back then for me was make me a bit out of it, really hungry, and then really tired.

So I was not sure if I should accept Kelly's invite but decided, what the heck, if I was going to die of chicken pox I would rather be a bit out of it and well-fed, so I said, "Let's go, light 'er up." It was dark by then, and Kelly said Elena had gone to bed early with a headache. She had given Kelly a key to the house in case we wanted to go in and cook up some dinner.

We climbed up to the balcony of our little casita and I have to admit, the stars were AMAZING! We both wondered why we had not gone up there before. As Kelly lit the joint I had a realization that I was *soooooooooo* glad she was there at that moment. I took one puff of the joint and before I knew it, I had launched into the whole story about the chicken pox and the little boy hurting his knee and the rose he made and how I was practically throwing pesos at the little kids just to keep them from coming near me and how I was sure my calling was to work at the orphanage but after that incident I was not so sure and how I realized I was not another Mother Teresa, to which Kelly blurted out in hysterics, "YOU!? Mother Teresa!?"

We were both rolling in hysterics at the whole thing. This pot must have been WAY better than the junk we had back in high school, because we kept doing that thing high people do where you are in the middle of a story and then your mind wanders off and you find yourself appreciating the color of your shirt more than you ever have appreciated anything in life and then you stop and say, "Sh*t, what were we talking about again?" and before you know it two hours have passed.

We laughed hysterically into the moon that night like a couple of lobos (wolves), and then Kelly suggested that we re-enact my whole day – she playing the various roles of the priest, the group leader, the little boy, the kids, while I played myself the whole time. Once again we found ourselves laughing so hard our stomachs hurt. Kelly then told me about her night with Enrique and the boys. By this time we had a bottle of wine open, and I will admit it, I had a cigarette in my mouth as Kelly told me the story of how she accidentally made Enrique and Elena think she was pregnant.

In Spanish the word "contenta" translates to the adjective "content," just like the word "computadora" translates to the noun "computer," "lampara" means "lamp" and so forth. So it is not out of the realm of possibility to assume that the word "embarazada" translates to what? "Embarassed," of course. Easy-peasy, right?

Wrong. This is where languages can be trippy. There are always the exceptions. For example, in English the word "tough" is pronounced "tuff," and the word "rough" is pronounced "ruff." But what about the word "though" – is it pronounced "thuff"? No, it is not. Case in point. There are always the exceptions. So here is what happened to Kelly and the word "embarazada."

"Embarazada" in Spanish actually means "pregnant." Who would think it? You would think pregnant would be "pregnanta" or something like that, but don't be fooled. So Kelly explained to me that on the car ride home that morning, after a very similar night to the previous outing with Enrique and his friends (one filled with crazy car rides, a party, some dancing, some toasts and a view of the sunrise from yet another spectacular place), Kelly had her head on José's shoulder and was a bit wasted. She began to say that she was embarrassed (about being so drunk), but she wanted to impress her newfound tutor with her Spanish so she took a stab at translating the word "embarrassed" on her own.

She began to babble on about how she was, "embarazada y borracha," which translated to "pregnant and drunk." She then asked José for a cigarette. He looked at Enrique in the mirror and Enrique returned a look as if to say "WTF?" Well, Kelly kept repeating how drunk and pregnant she was and if only someone would give her a damn cigarette she would feel better. You see how things can get SO lost in translation? By the time they dropped Kelly off, Enrique had decided it might be best to consult mom on this particular situation.

Elena was already up making coffee when Enrique brought Kelly in and said that it might be best for Kelly to talk to a woman about her problem. At this point Kelly was totally confused, but happy when Elena pulled out her cigarettes and she finally got what she had been asking for. Enrique took the cigarette out of her mouth and broke it in two before she could light it, explaining to poor, confused Elena that this Americana was pregnant.

Elena took a step back and looked at Kelly's stomach and said in English, "Pregnant?"

Kelly, who was confused as hell at this point, said, "What? Pregnant? Who?"

"YOU!" Enrique exclaimed. "You said in the car about ten times that you were pregnant, 'embarazada,' WITH CHILD!" He gestured awkwardly at her stomach. Kelly, still confused and quickly sobering up, racked her brain trying to figure out what was going on.

Then it clicked. "Oh… damn…! How do you say 'embarrassed' in Spanish?" she asked Elena.

Elena, whose English was so-so, had to have Kelly repeat the word a couple of times and then describe it. It was like a game of charades for about five minutes until finally Enrique cried, "Ahhhhh… avergonzada! Like you have shame!"

"Yes, yes! Much shame!" said Kelly. "I have much shame."

"Ahhhh…" piped in Elena. "So, no baby? No baby in belly? Just shame?" she asked, putting her hand on Kelly's stomach.

"Yes, I mean, no! No baby!" laughed Kelly. "Just shame."

"Well then…" said Elena, taking another cigarette and handing it to Kelly, "have your cigarette, you poor thing."

Kelly took the cigarette.

"You scared her, Enriquito!" Elena said, razzing her son, who was blushing. "Don't scare my girls, mi hijo!" she continued coolly, taking a puff of her cigarette.

They all laughed as they drank coffee. Suddenly Enrique realized poor José was still waiting for him in the car, which caused laughter again. Kelly walked Enrique out, and as they said good-bye he discreetly handed her the joint and said with a smile, "For the stress I may have caused."

So THAT is the story of the joint and how Kelly made Enrique and Elena think she was preggers. We laughed hysterically at how both our adventures had led us to that moment, sitting on the balcony under the stars and the big Mexican moon. It then hit both of us how ravenously hungry we were. It was nearly midnight by the then. We went to the house and quietly let ourselves in with the key Elena had given us. Elena had left us each a plate of food – one that said "sin carne" (without meat) and one that said "con carne" (with meat). We heated them up in the microwave and took them back to our room where we finished the wine and talked about how next weekend was a three-day weekend and how we should travel somewhere.

"Ah!" said Kelly. "Enrique said that he and the guys would be going to see Popocatépetl and we could come if we want."

"Popo copa… what-a-whatal?" I said, confused by the gibberish she seemed to be uttering.

"The volcano, Popo," she said, chewing a bite of her sandwich. Then she taught me how to say the full name.

"Po-po-ca-ta-pet-el." After about five tries I finally got it right. Kelly explained that Popo was an eruptive volcano not too far from Mexico City. We got out our travel book and looked it up. We learned that the volcano was located in the states of Puebla and Morelos, about forty-five miles from Mexico City. How cool is that? We lived about an hour away from an active volcano! Talk about going from extreme cold to potentially extreme heat!

Kelly went on to read that, "'Popocatépetl is one of the most active volcanoes in Mexico, having produced more than fifteen major eruptions since the Spanish arrived in 1519. A major one occurred in 1947. Most recently, in December of 1994, after the volcano spewed gas and ash causing the evacuation of nearby towns, scientists began monitoring for another major eruption.'" As we were reading we were munching on the dinner Elena made for us. I went to take a bite of the sandwich she had made and realized that I was eating the "sin carne" one (the one without meat). I looked over at Kelly's plate and saw that the only thing left on it was a few crumbs. She had eaten the whole "con carne" (with meat) sandwich and had not even noticed! I debated whether to tell her or not and then decided I just had to.

"Girl," I said. She looked up at me from the book. "Do you realize you just ate a whole meat sandwich?"

She looked down at her plate. "Noooo… I didn't… did I?"

We were both still pretty lit from the joint and the half a bottle of wine, and we both busted out laughing once she realized it was true. Sprawled on our little beds, we laughed hysterically. Then Kelly looked at me and said, "Girl," and I said "What?" and she said, "You do realize you are still alive, right? You have not died from chicken pox?" and once again we burst out laughing until we were holding our stomachs.

"Now let's just hope we survive the volcano!" I said, and as we laughed about it we got ready for bed and both passed when our heads hit our pillows. I did not wake once, and am not sure if Kelly snored that night or not because I was so tired and knocked out from the day's events and the night's "festivities."

The next day when I awoke I realized how thankful I was for Kelly. Had she not been there the previous evening to distract me from my "chicken pox" debacle, I am sure I would have convinced myself I had the pox until I manifested them by pure worry or I would have been in such a panic I would have convinced myself to go back to Minnesota for fear of dying in some under-qualified Mexican hospital (which to be honest, on-the-contrary, would probably provide better care than a hospital here in the U.S. and for less cost!)

Chapter Fourteen

That week flew by and I realized that I had better appreciate everything I could, because a couple of months do go pretty fast when you think about it. The classes we took required for the most part a lot of out-loud reading, memorizing, and some writing. On our bus rides to and from school Kelly and I would quiz each other on vocabulary words. For our writing class we had to keep a journal and write solely in Spanish. Class time was generally dedicated to reading aloud. The professor would stop students when necessary and have them repeat words they were having trouble with (like "enfo-car," you remember the word "enfocar"). I felt like I was progressing well, but I still found that rolling my 'r's was particularly troublesome. I was told that with time and practice it would come.

Rolling your 'r's in Spanish is important because some words are distinguished by the sound of a rolling 'r' as opposed to your plain, old normal 'r'. Rolled 'r's are signified by two 'r's in a row. For example, the word "pero" means "but," while the word "perro" means dog. "Carro" means "car" and "caro" means "expensive." I still have trouble sometimes with it, even after earning a Master's degree in Spanish, and if you think it is easy to change your speech patterns overnight, think about this. In English we have a similar thing. You ever talk to someone from the south? One of my great aunts lives in Texas, and one time my mom was there for a visit. My great aunt asked my mom to run to the store and pick up some "All" and some other items. So my mom came home with a box of All laundry detergent along with the other items my great aunt requested. My great aunt asked her where the "All" was. My mom, confused as hell, pointed at the box of detergent. My great-aunt opened the cupboard and pulled out a nearly empty plastic bottle of cooking oil and said, "Not ALL... *ALL!*"

Now, try to get Great Aunt So-and-So from Texas to say "oil" instead of "all" and it does not happen overnight, let me tell you! Ask anyone from Boston to say the word "harp" and you will hear "hop," or someone from New York to say "talk" and they say "twock." So my point is, the way we speak is hard to change over a short period of time, and I have decided to give myself some slack on the whole rolling the 'r' thing.

On a quasi-related point, since we are talking about languages; once, a couple of years ago in a yoga class I was taking, a teacher told the class something that actually made a lot of sense about why Latinos can dance so well (you know those Latinos and their loose hips). He explained that it has to do with the fact that Latino's roll their 'r's when they talk. Now this of course fascinated me, since I had studied Spanish and had trouble with rolling my 'r's as well as the fact that, after years of salsa dancing, I still have trouble swiveling my hips. What can I say, I have a lot of German and Irish in me; I am as white as they come! Anyway, he explained that when a person rolls their 'r's the tip of their tongue hits a spot behind the front teeth that connects to and stimulates certain energy points in the pelvis and hip area, which is why Latinos are so much more loose in the hips (and are just more sensual in general). It made sense to me and stuck! I just wonder if the faster one speaks (and the faster they roll their 'r's), the more swivelly their hips are, because Puerto Ricans definitely speak Spanish extremely fast and have some of the most swivelly hips I have ever seen!

So, getting back to our week. Kelly and I would practice rolling 'r's on the bus rides home. It really helped to have her, and I felt that the night on the balcony was just the bonding experience we had needed. She did, however, continue to snore. And this is where I had to make a tough decision. Telling her was out of the question as far as I was concerned. It would only make me feel bad and her feel bad, and I did not want to have to pretend that there was something wrong at Elena's that would cause me to request a change. So on Monday night, after Kelly fell asleep and just when she started doing the Cement Truck, I decided that I was going to risk sleeping in the house.

We still had the key that Elena had given us, and she actually said we should keep it just in case we ever needed to get inside for some reason. Well, I needed to get inside so that I would not end up behind bars for life, and felt that was reason enough! I figured if I were caught I would just say that I felt really ill and went inside to heat some water up for tea and sat down on the couch for a minute and just ended up falling asleep. She always had an extra afghan on the couch so I could curl up in that. The only thing that worried me was what if, as I was entering, she thought the place was being burglarized? What if she had a gun? What if she came out in the middle of the night and saw me and had a heart attack?

I could see the headlines on this one: "American Student Accidentally Shot by Mexican Host Mother." All these questions made this decision a really tough one.

I knew that Elena's room was situated in the back of the house and that she most likely would not hear me. I also figured if she did hear the door open she would assume it was one of us. I went on debating about this for about fifteen minutes, and when Kelly's snoring turned into the Delores Claiborne I decided it was worth taking a chance and sneaking into the house. Ever so carefully I tiptoed my way out the door, taking my alarm clock and my pillow. It was a cinch. As I lay down I began thinking about how funny it all was that I had to take refuge because of someone's snoring. I most likely ended up falling asleep with a big ol' smirk on my face.

My alarm woke me at 5:45 a.m. – plenty of time to sneak back into the cottage. I knew Kelly was one of those people who hit snooze on their alarm clock about five times and would push it until about 6:15 each morning. I tiptoed in, dropped my pillow on my bed, and headed straight in to the shower. It felt SO great to have gotten a solid night's sleep. When I came out of the shower Kelly was just turning off her alarm and moaning that she was getting up in five minutes.

I have to say it was kind of fun to have a little secret. Each night that week I did the same thing. At about 10:15 I would sneak into the house. By then Elena was in her room sleeping and Kelly was just beginning one of her snores. I even made a fun little game out of it all, and would try and guess what snore she would do before I made my nightly escape. The Andy Griffith seemed to be popular that first week.

Needless to say I had not contracted chicken pox, and I had to laugh at myself for being so hysterical about it at the orphanage that past Saturday. In fact, I had completely forgotten about the whole thing until someone brought it up in one of my classes. They asked if I had felt like I had any signs of falling ill, and I said, "Luckily not!" I chuckled to myself thinking about how Kelly and I re-enacted the whole thing, and how the laughter that we got out of the experience almost made it all worth it.

That Tuesday's excursion to Mexico City allowed students to visit the Frida Kahlo Museum, or the Casa Azul ("Blue House"). Now, the only thing I had known about Frida Kahlo up until that point was she was not ashamed of that uni-brow she always sported, and why should she be? Look at Brooke Shields, for crying out loud! Again, another very pointed reason as to why it is essential to break out of the bubble and travel. There was so much to learn about this fascinating woman besides the fact that she had no interest whatsoever in wasting her time plucking her eyebrows – a true feminist and a heroine to all women in my book. Why, just because *Glamour* magazine says it is in style to draw in your thinly plucked eyebrows, should women waste time and energy on such a silly and painful process while they could spend their time becoming a revolutionary artist like Frida?

Upon arriving at "The Blue House", which literally is a blue stucco-like house with a green door, orange trim, and green and white windows, I was immediately amazed. All I can say is, this house ROCKED! It was then and there that I decided if I ever owned a home, it would have to be unique like this one. Years later (and it is still one of my dreams) I saw a book about earth houses, primarily constructed from mud-adobe and recycled items like rubber tires for insulation and glass bottles for decoration and light, and thought that maybe someday one of those would be my very own version of the Blue House.

As we herded our way through the little blue home and modern day museum, we learned that Frida's life began and ended in Mexico City, in that very same blue house. Our excursion leader pointed out that she gave her birth date as July 7, 1910, but her birth certificate actually shows July 6, 1907. He went on to explain that, "Kahlo had supposedly wanted her birth year to align with the beginning of the Mexican revolution in 1910 so that her life would also commence with the birth of modern Mexico." Wow, now that is living with intention, which is another valuable thing I believe people get from traveling and really seeing how the world works. Instead of floating along and living as if we have no choice in our surroundings, when we travel we may see and experience a way of life much different from what we know or find familiar, allowing us to make changes and to be more open when change inevitably occurs.

We learned that Kahlo's art has been praised in Mexico as being symbolic of national and indigenous tradition, and by feminists for its "uncompromising depiction of the female experience and form." Not to harp on the issue, but just look at those un-plucked eyebrows and you can't argue with that latter statement.

As we finished our tour of the museum, I read on the information sheet the guide handed us that "a few days before Frida Kahlo died on July 13, 1954, she wrote in her diary: 'I hope the exit is joyful – and I hope never to return

– Frida.'" The official cause of death was given as pulmonary embolism. What an honest woman!

While riding back to the school on the bus that day, I thought about the impact Frida Kahlo had on the world with her art – and on the feminist movement. It made me wonder what impact I could potentially have as well, and I was brought back to the image of Yesenia and the little girls in the Zocolo. I still felt like the experience was not something I would ever forget about. I thought about little Yesenia and the other girls and all the kids at the orphanage, and knew I was meant to do something in my life differently because of them. I was just not sure what it was – not just yet.

Chapter Fifteen

Enrique phoned us mid-week to see if we still planned on going camping with him, José, and Javier over the long weekend ahead. We confirmed plans, and as we began to pack Kelly and I quizzed each other on vocabulary words for that week. Each Thursday we had a vocabulary test, and we would spend Wednesday evenings questioning each other. I had to admit it never got old – learning new words. We were also learning grammar and sentence structure. This is something I never remember having learned in English class as a kid and why I still find myself appreciative that I learned a second language as an adult. When you are a kid you just sort of memorize things and learn them by rote – that is why they say kids learn languages so fast – they don't ask why, they just do.

By the time Friday arrived, Kelly and I were ready for another chance to admire the stars and let loose a bit. I had had a whole week of solid sleep each night and was feeling ready for an adventure! We packed our warmest clothes because we were told that at night the temperatures dropped to about 30 degrees. During the day they would climb up to the 90's, so we made sure to bring shorts and tank tops. We both brought hiking boots, sandals, thick socks, our warmest jackets, sweaters, and Elena lent us a couple extra pairs of long underwear, hats, and gloves. Enrique would supply the camping gear and said he would also supply the food if we pitched in for gas. We were set to go and see our first volcano, and so after our breakfast we went back to our cottage and brought out our bags to wait for Enrique and the boys to show up.

They were right on time and had even brought us some coffees to go. Once again I had one of those moments where I could not believe this was my life. I could not believe that at that very moment I could have been back in Minnesota dealing with trying to figure out the snow plow schedule, which is more confusing than advanced algebra; and if you do not believe me, I have cut, copied and pasted a sample of the rules from the Minneapolis, City of Lakes, official website explaining the whole thing just so you can see with your very own eyes what I am talking about:

> Day 1: 9 p.m. to 8 a.m. (overnight). Do not park on either side of the street with the red sign: Snow Emergency Route. Snowplows will clear those streets first. A Snow Emergency will be declared no later than 6 p.m. on any given day. At 9 p.m. on that day, Snow Emergency parking rules begin. Park on either side of non-Snow Emergency routes (these streets DO NOT have the red sign: Snow Emergency Route). On the first day it snows, known as 'day one' after a street is fully plowed, feel free to park there, even if Snow Emergency parking rules are still in effect. Fully plowed means the street is completely cleared and plowed as wide as possible. Plows may come through more than once, so make sure that it is fully plowed as wide as possible before parking.

Day 2: 8 a.m. to 8 p.m. Day Two parking rules begin. Do not park on the EVEN side of non-Snow Emergency routes. (Example: house address number: 1356 Maple or 2512 17th Ave.) Do not park on either side of parkways. Park on the odd side of non-Snow Emergency Route streets (example: house address number 1359 Maple or 2513 17th Ave.). Park on either side of streets with the red sign: Snow Emergency Route.).

Day 3: 8 a.m. to 8 p.m. At 8 a.m., Day Three parking rules begin. Do not park on the ODD side of non-Snow Emergency Route streets (example: house address number 1359 or 2513 17th Ave.). Park on even side of non-Snow Emergency Route streets. (Example: house address number: 1356 Maple or 2512 17th Ave.) Park on either side of streets marked with the red sign: Snow Emergency Route and you may park on parkways. After a street is fully plowed, feel free to park there, even if Snow Emergency parking rules are still in effect. Fully plowed means the street is completely cleared and plowed as wide as possible. Plows may come through more than once, so make sure that it is fully plowed as wide as possible before parking.

You see what I am saying? And here is the thing: if you get confused on the rules, which is easy to do, you end up either having your car towed or you end up shoveling your car out of some ridiculous snow bank turned to ice already. I know because I have dealt with both situations a number of times in my years of winter survival. So like I said, I could not believe I was in Mexico, on my way to see a volcano, with a group of people I never would have met before, and as Enrique turned up the radio and the boys let out a loud "YEEEEHAAAAAW!" we all burst out laughing and did a toast with our coffees: "To Popo!"

Along the way we discussed the plan for the weekend. We would arrive early enough to get in a solid hike that day, but before embarking on the hike we would have to figure out our campsite. Javier read from a guidebook he had that Popo was surrounded by a national park called the Iztaccihuatl-Popocatépetl National Park. The park was created in 1935. He went on to read in his almost perfect English (with a slight accent which sounded so endearing to the ear it made him even sexier than Ryan Gosling):

"'The sylvan flora and fauna of the park are of nearctic and neotropical origin. In its geographic location it forms a part of the trans-Mexican volcanic zone, enabling it to have a great diversity of habitats, such as mixed forests of pine and evergreen oak as well as high mountain prairies.'"

"*Coooooool!* I can't wait to smell the pine!" Kelly exclaimed, clapping her hands in delight.

Javier took a sip of his coffee and continued to read. "'Alpine habitats can be found at the highest altitudes, a great rarity in Mexico as the country is located in the sub-tropical zone. These forests house nearly a thousand species of plants, comprising forty percent of the reported species in the Valley of Mexico.'"

"Wow!" I said, squeezing Kelly's knee. "I can't believe this!"

Javier continued. "'For its part, the fauna is an extraordinary richness of species, including mammals such as the zacatuche or teporingo rabbit, the puma, the lynx, the coati and the white-tailed deer, which constitute forty percent of registered mammals in the Sierra Nevada. Also, the volcanic corridor serves as a resting point for diverse species of birds on their migratory routes to the Gulf and the Pacific.'"

"Wow!" Javier stopped reading. "Dude, I do *not* think I want to camp with puma!"

We all laughed. Then the car became quiet as we each contemplated the idea of actually camping among all the wild animals Javier had just checked off. After another moment of silence, where it became clear someone was going to say something like, "Are we sure we want to do this?" I asked, "Are we sure we can even camp there? Does the book say anything about camp sites?"

"People do it all the time," said Enrique. "Don't worry."

"DON'T WORRY!?" I thought, and I was right back in my chicken-pox panic mode where I was kicking myself for not having read more about this whole idea of camping near this damn volcano.

All of a sudden I found myself angry at Kelly and her stupid joint the other night which had made me so high that I had convinced myself to just go with the flow and roam when in Rome and all that bull. Now I was most likely going to die with this group of morons and be eaten by a frickin' puma. I felt my anxiety grow until José lit up a cigarette. I asked for a drag of it to calm my nerves. I asked to see the book and began reading to myself. I discovered that there was a hotel, The Hotel San Carlos, not far from the park and that on the park grounds there were two lodges. One of the lodges was actually where the scientists who were monitoring the volcano lived and the other one could be rented for the evening.

I told everybody what I had read and said that I thought we should check out the hotel or the lodge because, to be honest, I was freaking out. Enrique laughed and said I should not worry. "People do it all the time," he said for the second time, to which I responded, "Yeah, well, people do a lot of stupid stuff all the time, but it doesn't mean I am going to do it. You guys can sleep in tents, but I am checking out the hotel or the lodge."

Javier then piped in and said, "I am with her. Like I said, I am not sure if I am up for spooning with a puma all night, not to mention a lynx." He chuckled uneasily, his green eyes darting in my direction.

"Well, I am up for camping," declared Kelly defiantly, and Enrique and José chimed in that they were also up for camping.

"I think you guys are making kind of a big deal about the whole thing," said José. "Honestly, my cousin did it last year and was fine. He said the stars were amazing and you only live once, you know?"

"Exactly," I said. "You only live once, and I want to live as long as I can!" I then added lightly, "Look, if you guys want to camp, camp. But I honestly feel better staying inside somewhere. That is just my preference – go and camp with the puma and the lynx if you feel like it is what you want to do."

"We're not going to get eaten by a lynx," Kelly said, annoyed. "I wish you would just lighten up," she snapped at me. With all the talking, none of us had really been paying attention to the sights around us and suddenly Enrique said, "Hey guys… look ahead… it's Popo."

We all stopped talking and peered through the windshield, and there it was – Popo. I had NEVER seen anything like it in my life. I mean, I had seen Mount Shasta, which is amazing, but there was something so alive about Popo. I mean, duh, it *is* an active volcano, but you could see even from a distance that it was almost like a sleeping giant, just waiting to be awakened.

It looked like an enormous mountain covered in tin foil with snow at the top. It was glassy and shimmery, not what I expected. With its silver sheen it reminded me of a large, cone shaped nuclear bomb. I thought it was going to be brown, black, and dirty looking – but it was smooth as ice and shiny. To say the least it was completely impressive.

"HOLY MOLY" said Kelly. "I am DEFINITELY camping as close to that thing as possible!"

I just kept my mouth shut but thought to myself, "… and I am DEFINITELY staying as far *away* from that thing as possible!"

As we got closer to the park entrance we saw the hotel coming up on our right. I asked Enrique to pull over so I could inquire if they had any rooms. Pretty much everyone had to use the restroom by that point, so nobody put up a fight. I inquired with the man at the front desk if they had any rooms. It was clear he did not speak a lick of English, so Javier jumped in and quickly found out that no, there were no vacancies, but that the lodge in the park was available. We asked if we could use the hotel phone to call, and he explained that we should just show up there and would most likely run into one of the scientists at the lodge.

So we made our way to the park entrance. There was nobody in the booth, but a hanging sign indicated where to leave our money and provided instructions for completing the little form we needed to fill out with the license plate number of our car. The area looked desolate, and the sign looked like it had been there for a while, all weathered and beaten up. I wondered if maybe a puma had eaten the attendant and nobody knew, because honestly there was not a soul in sight. All that loomed ahead was Popo. I was happy to know, though, that at least there was a hotel not so far away and I would sleep on the damn reservations counter if I had to in order to avoid camping out in this eerie, desolate place. As we forged ahead down a bumpy road of dirt, I wondered if we would even come across anybody else along the way at all.

There were no other cars in sight and I could not yet see the lodge. I did have to admit that as we drove I could appreciate the beauty of the park. Trees surrounded a large field of green grass that seemed to make its way up to the bottom of Popo. Green grass as far as the eye could see. White and yellow flowers grew like a patchwork quilt with occasional purple ones spattered in between. It looked like an amazing jigsaw puzzle picture of some scene that I would never see with my own eyes, but here I was. I was actually here – seeing it with my very own eyes.

It was a surreal feeling to be in the presence of such an incredible work of God and nature and to be surrounded by only four other people. No malls, no cars, no stoplights, no pedestrians, no billboards, no honking horns, no nothing – just the green grass God made and this volcano. How out of the box can you get? Oh, and, somewhere in the trees and brush were pumas, lynx, some kind of Mexican rabbits I could not remember the names of, and a handful of other creatures. As I breathed in the clean, cool air that wafted in through the open windows of Enrique's car, my anxiety began to ease. As we got closer to the mountain I did start to make out the two lodges the man at the hotel told us about.

They were pretty much your typical lodges, all wood and both fairly small in size. I imagined the scientists in one of them with all their scientific equipment – seismograph machines and dashboards with all sorts of knobs and lights that somehow would alert them if there were any changes in the volcano. It was pretty damn cool, I had to say. As we approached the lodges I could see a vehicle parked outside one of them, and I felt even more relief, assuming we would meet the scientists and could secure a spot at the lodge. As we parked and got out of the vehicle a man came out of the lodge. He was very dark skinned and almost looked indigenous. Enrique spoke right away as the man approached.

"Hola, ¿Hablas Español o Nahuatl?" he asked ("Do you speak Spanish or Nahuatl?"). In one of our classes we had learned that Nahuatl (Ipronounced "nah-wah-tel") was the language of the Aztecs who had dominated what is now central Mexico during the late Postclassic period of Mesoamerican history and has been spoken in Central Mexico since at least the 7th century A.D.

Today a number of versions of the language are spoken in various communities scattered mostly in rural areas throughout central Mexico and along the coastline. The man approaching our car was a scientist, who we learned was named Amoxtli, and he said he spoke a little bit of Spanish but mostly Nahautl. He told us to call him Amox, and asked how he could help us. Enrique explained that two members of our party would like to stay in the lodge for the next two nights. He pointed at Javier and me and we both waved.

Amox told us they charged the equivalent of $20.00 a night. There was running water but no hot water and that was it as far as amenities. There was not even a bathroom, just a sink. Javier and I each quickly handed over our respective halves of the money.

"¿Y usted y lo otros dos? ¿Dónde van a quedarse para la noche?" ("And you and the other two, where will you be staying for the night?") inquired Amox.

Enrique said they would be camping out under the stars. When Amox heard this he began to chuckle and said, "Ten cuidado, Yo sé que a los jóvenes les gustan a acampar afuera, pero con cuidado, ¿eh? ("Be careful, I know that the youngsters like to camp outside, but with care, eh?")

Amox then showed us up to the lodge. The door was locked, but he gave us a key and said to slide it under the door of the other lodge when we left. I had to say that Amox was not what I expected. When someone says "scientist" the image that comes to my mind is someone with a white lab coat or some kind of vest with a lot of pockets and measuring devices and a pen behind his or her ear and a little notepad tucked in one pocket and a pocket protector in the other pocket with a magnifying glass and some type of little set of tools – and this is yet another reason it is important to get out of the box! Amox had none of these things. His hair was long and in a braid going down his back. He was wearing a very heavy coat and pants and work boots, but no pocket protector. He had a long mustache and a beard. I noticed a silver and black ring on his finger and wondered if he was married. Did he have kids? What about his parents? I was fascinated, and I felt *soooooooo* relieved that I was going to be staying in a lodge. It didn't matter if it had hot water or not, it had walls, a roof, and a door that shut!

I was also relieved that Javier would be staying with me. I had brought a deck of cards and some flashlights and candles, and I thought maybe it would be fun after a day of hiking to come back and play a little "War" before going to bed. As Enrique, Javier and I unloaded the vehicle, Kelly and José looked at the guidebook, mapping out the best way to reach the foot of the volcano.

Finally we were ready to set off on the hike. The temperature was about 65 degrees already, so we crammed sweatshirts, water, food and cameras into our backpacks and got our hiking boots on. Enrique, Kelly, and José were still set on camping that evening and brought their tent, camping stove, sleeping bags and lanterns. As we set out on the hike, Enrique pulled a joint out and lit it. We passed it around, taking a couple puffs each as we walked along the trail created by others who had gone before us.

Chapter Sixteen

It was incredible walking towards the volcano. I felt like Dorothy in *The Wizard of Oz* as she and the lion, the scarecrow, the tin man, and Toto made their way through the poppy fields to the Emerald City. Each step brought us a little closer to standing beneath this amazing wonder. At first I was not going to partake in any puffs off the joint, but as we trudged on I felt that it might calm my nerves and decided one or two puffs would be okay. I have to admit that as well as calming my nerves it intensified the colors and smells and sounds of the hike in a way that made me feel like I was floating through the fields of green and white and yellow and purple instead of walking.

The temperature soon hit ninety degrees and we were not even half way to the foot of the volcano. Enrique and José were switching off carrying the big pack with the camping gear, and Javier took it a couple times as well. We stopped to drink water and have snacks, and at one point Kelly said she was going to just leave her backpack and hike hands-free for a bit. "There is nobody else out here," she said "I will just pick it up on our way back down."

We were all feeling the heat and her plan actually did seem to make sense, so we decided we would leave everything except one bag in which we carried our water and cameras, snacks, lunch, and one guidebook. There really was not another person in sight. We left everything in an organized pile and took a stick and tied one of Enrique's red shirts to it so we would be able to see it coming back. We were essentially hiking through a huge green field, so just in case we got off track we at least flagged where we left everything. It was like we were explorers leaving a trail behind us.

At about noon we sat down to eat some lunch. The guidebook said that back in the 1970's people were actually able to hike up the volcano because it was not active then. Now, the farthest we would get would be to the base because there was a big fence that prevented anyone from going too close. It was so incredible, and the closer we got the happier I was that I was on this adventure. It really was spectacular.

As we ate lunch, Kelly brought up the fact that the volcano could really erupt at any point. Then José brought up the fact that that is why the scientists were there, and had they noticed any signs of an impending eruption they would have stopped us from hiking. That thought was reassuring enough for me to relax and just enjoy the adventure.

We saw several deer along the way and a lot of birds, but did not see anything else at that point. We made a game – the first person to see a rabbit would not have to carry the bag the whole time – until then we switched it every so often. The sun beat down on us, and I was happy I had brought a hat. It felt great to get a workout on the legs, and after lunch we did a little stretching and then got on our way.

We walked in silence for a little over an hour until we saw a sign that said Popocatépetl Baseline in one mile. One mile! But the volcano still seemed so far away. We decided to stop for some water and to read the guidebook a little more. It said that the baseline was set at one mile from the base of the volcano – so essentially we were two miles away from the foot of the volcano. It made me feel better knowing that we were not actually going to be standing at the bottom of a volcano, but everyone else seemed pretty bummed out.

"I was hoping to touch the volcano," Kelly whined. "Oh well, it still is cool!" she said, and got up and did a cartwheel. It looked fun so I stood up and did one too.

The guys laughed and began to run, yelling "Yeeeeehaaaaw!" José did something that sort of looked like a cartwheel, and Javier did a somersault. We laughed and were all giddy to be so close to the final destination. We arrived at the baseline a half an hour later. It was AMAZING to be that close, and to look up and see this glassy, blue and silver volcano with its white top peering down at us. It looked like it had changed shades from when we first started our hike. It was like a giant mood ring – I just hoped it would stay in a good mood until we got safely back to Cuernavaca. Needless to say, we took a ton of pictures by the sign that read, "Do not cross! Active Volcano!" and of course José had to have a picture showing him trying to climb the fence, and we set up the camera to take a group picture.

Enrique had brought some pulque so we had a ceremonial toast to Popo and the pumas. We shared a smoke and then decided to do one last group photo before leaving the baseline. I noticed Javier was right by my side, and just as we were about to say "cheecha!" (which is "whiskey" in Spanish), he pulled me near and whispered in my ear, "Tonight is going to be fun," and he gave me a little peck on my cheek and then dashed off to grab the backpack. "Vamanos!" he yelled joyfully and he ran ahead and we all followed in suit, waving good-bye to Popo.

On the way back I was focused on what had just happened with Javier. He really was a looker with that blonde hair and his green eyes. I tried to think back to the very brief time we spent time together. When we all went out to the party that one Saturday night he did not seem to be hanging on women. When we danced he was very courteous and was not checking out girls left and right, and when I thought about it he did sit next to me in the vehicle on the ride there, and even insisted he do so, saying he wanted Kelly to have a window view. I thought about him reading out loud and how sweet his English was. He looked back at me once and winked. I smiled back and gave a wave. Nobody noticed.

The hike was about three and a half hours, and for the most part we all chatted about this bird or that flower, and then José, who was carrying the bag, said he SWORE he saw a rabbit and handed the backpack to Kelly. He then ran off and broke out laughing, admitting he actually had not seen the rabbit, he just did want to carry the bag anymore. Then he pulled Kelly in for a hug and took the backpack back. He kissed her cheek and they just laughed and began to toss the bag back and forth. Enrique walked ahead with a walking stick he had picked up somewhere along the way. He passed back the bottle of pulque and we all stopped for a rest.

As we began walking again, Javier came from behind me and offered me a flower. Okay, this was *toooooo* much! I giggled to myself.

"Para ti, mi flor" ("For you, my flower"), he said with a smile and a wink. I was completely smitten and blushing all over the place, and then he said to me in English, "Tonight maybe we can have another dance under the moon," to which I stuttered, "Yes, I would love that."

I mean, how lame was that? Could I not have said anything cleverer? And then the words fell out of my mouth. "You know how much I like to spin around."

He said back with a wink, "Oh, I will spin you around – I will spin your world around." Then he pulled me close and kissed my neck.

Okay, okay. Now, I had been around the block enough times to detect a guy who just wants to get in a girl's pants, and let me tell you, the red flags shot up as soon as he did this. And the whole "spin your world around" set off a couple more red flags. Not to mention the winking and the premature neck kiss. I mean, really? And what was with him calling me his flower? Listen up, ladies; if you meet a guy and he calls you his flower, tells you he is going to spin your world around, and kisses you anywhere prematurely, you may be better off sleeping in the wild with a puma lurking outside your tent. And this was exactly the predicament I was in now. I was stuck between sleeping outside with pumas or inside with frickin' Don Juan, for crying out loud. Once again anxiety struck. All my stuff was back at the lodge – my sleeping bag, my warmest clothes, my hat, long underwear – all the things I would need to stay warm enough to last through the night if I decided it would be better to just camp.

And after all the red flags that seemed to be popping up all over the place, I really did not want to be alone with Javier in that lodge all night. My instincts were telling me that he was most likely harmless, but still.... I figured I could pull Kelly aside and tell her what was going on – but then I also figured she would tell me not to worry and stop being such a panicky Jane. I decided to walk next to Enrique for a bit and see if somehow I could talk him out of camping and coming back to the lodge. We walked along admiring all the different flowers and birds, and he began to tell me that the last time he went hiking was with his father.

"Ahhh...." I said.

"He always walked with a walking stick he would find along the way," he chuckled, reminiscing fondly. "I am so sorry he has passed."

After a pause I asked, "When did it happen?" feeling like he wanted to talk about it.

"About five years ago. From cancer," he said.

"Ohhh... I am so sorry."

"Well, we all go from something. It was really hard on mi mama," he said. "They were so in love their whole marriage."

"Yeah," I said. "She talks about him a lot."

"Well, here is to mi papa," he said, and lifted his walking stick in the air.

"Yes," I said. "To your papa."

There was an awkward silence, and just as I was about to bring up the subject of not camping, José, out of the blue, said, "Hey! Do you see up there? There is an animal...what is it?"

We all stopped. Masking the sun from my eyes with my hand, I saw the animal, and then I saw a couple more. They were way off in the distance and seemed to not be running or even really moving.

"Are they bears?" José asked, squinting. We stopped and Enrique pulled out a small pair of binoculars from the bag.

"They're bulls," he said in an almost astonished tone.

"Bulls?" Kelly said.

"Yeah, here, take a look." Enrique passed her the binoculars.

"Yep, they're bulls. Five of them, I think," she said, handing the binoculars to José.

Everyone took a peek through the binoculars, and by the time they got to me I noticed that one of the bulls had something red and brown hanging from one of its horns. "You guys, I think one of the bulls killed an animal or something. It looks like it has something bloody hanging from its horn."

"Is it a rabbit!?" asked José enthusiastically.

"Ummmm… I can't tell," I said. The bulls were too far for us to determine what the red and brown thing was, and so we resumed hiking.

"The book did not say anything about bulls," Enrique pointed out. "I mean, you would think it would have mentioned bulls."

"I am just glad they aren't bears," Kelly said as she took a drink of water from her water bottle.

"Bulls are vicious," said Javier, sidling up along me and pinching my waist and giving me another wink. By then I had already pretty much determined that this whole thing with Javier was just not going to happen. In a matter of minutes he went from Ryan Gosling to Ryan Seacrest in my book. Nothing makes a man lose his attractiveness like coming on too strong too fast in my book. Not to mention a guy with bad timing! I mean, being hit on while potentially witnessing a bull mowing down a helpless little baby Mexican rabbit is just plain tacky if you ask me.

As we got closer to the bulls though we realized they were very close to where we had left all our gear. Enrique, after looking through his binoculars, turned to us and said, "Ha! You know the red thing hanging from the bull's horn?"

We all stopped and no one said a word. "Let me guess, it is not a rabbit?" chided José. Nobody laughed.

"No, it is my t-shirt!" Enrique exclaimed with almost a laugh.

"What!?" we all shouted in unison, grabbing for the binoculars at the same time. Sure enough, the bulls had pretty much trampled over all our bags, and the biggest, meanest looking one of them all stood there staring at us with Enrique's t-shirt hanging from his horn.

"You know what happens when a bull sees red?" asked Javier, who was suddenly at my side. Now, I was not in the mood for whatever kind of move he was trying to put on me, but before I could answer the bull started walking towards us. He shook his head a bit, trying to get the shirt to unhook from his horn, but it would not detach.

"Oh no," Enrique muttered. There honestly was nothing between us and the bulls but green grass and flowers. We all started to walk backwards very, very slowly. The bull walked towards us as slowly as we retreated. I had to admit, if I had not been so freaked out at the moment I would have been chuckling at this fierce beast coming at us with that t-shirt dangling from his horn. I mean, as scary as bulls are, they do not have the advantage of the opposable thumb like humans have. Every now and again he would try to shake it off with a determined look, becoming more and more frustrated with each attempt. I actually felt bad for the bull and wished I could somehow help him unhook that damn t-shirt from his horn.

"Looks like Ferdinand wants to make friends with us," whispered Kelly.

"Who in the hell is Ferdinand?" José whispered back.

"You know, Ferdinand the Bull? Walt Disney?" she replied in a whisper. José looked blank faced. "The bull who liked to smell flowers all day long?" she went on. Nope, José had no clue. It seemed like she was going to keep trying to explain who Ferdinand the Bull was to José until I stopped her.

"I know who you are talking about," I whispered back.

"Love that one," she said. Enrique then shushed us and gestured for us to keep walking backwards very slowly.

The other bulls began to follow Ferdinand, who was apparently the leader of the group. My heart started beating fast. I thought how my dad used to ride in rodeos in his twenties. One of my favorite photos of him was on a bull, and there was a clown in the photo, too. "Damn, I wish we had a clown outfit right now," I thought to myself. "Maybe the bull senses that my dad rode in rodeos and he finally has his chance to seek revenge." Okay, my fear was now making me maybe a bit delirious. I was actually starting to feel like this was all just a funny dream. We all kept giving each other silent looks as if to ask, "WTF should we do?" We would all return the looks to each other with the same, "I have no effing idea! I have never been in this situation before" expression attached.

All of a sudden one of the bulls in the back of the group began to grind his front legs into one of the backpacks on the ground as if he were crushing it. He then dipped his head down, hooked the bag with his horn, and tossed the bag to the side.

"Well, looks like we won't be camping tonight. There went the tent," whispered José. I then began to think that maybe the bulls were angry because they thought we littered on their pristine land. Then it hit me that thankfully, if we made it out of this mess, we would all be staying at the lodge tonight.

The bull then did the same thing to an orange and green backpack. "I think that was your bag he just trampled, Kelly," whispered Javier.

This was getting ridiculous. I had to laugh to myself. For some reason, I am not sure if it was because I was so traumatized or what, I was not afraid. I felt an exhilaration just thinking about the whole situation. This was life! This was not a movie I was watching in some stinky, dingy movie theatre. This was real life: us out in the open, an active volcano looming in the background, bulls approaching... REAL LIFE! We were still slowly moving backwards. That was our plan, I guess, to just keep slowly walking backwards.

Then my mind jumped to what the headlines would read: "Group of American Study Abroad Students Trampled by Bulls while Hiking near an Active Volcano." Honestly, those were the types of headlines you'd read, and you'd find it hard to feel bad about because all you want to know is how stupid could these students be to end up wedged between wild bulls and an active volcano in the first place? I mean, really, right? Just being caught fleeing from one of these precarious situations is bad enough, but being stuck in between two of them!?

Then they would look at the pictures from our cameras and see José's dumb ass trying to climb over the fence with the sign that reads, "Stay Out – Active Volcano" and you could just hear the remarks: "Well, what can you expect?" or, "Well, survival of the fittest, you know? I mean, ya gotta weed out the idiots somehow, right?" or, "I do not even feel bad for them, how stupid must their parents have been to raise such morons?" So then not even our parents would receive any sympathy – just dirty looks.

Then I pictured my mom's face. This could not happen. My mom was a great mother. It was not her fault her daughter was such an idiot. Then I began to pray. And had I not been following the plan to just keep walking backwards, I would have been on my knees praying. And I mean REALLY praying. Not any of this, "I promise I will never do something this stupid again, Lord," type of praying, but the, "Lord, I am so scared I cannot even BS about this promise or that promise at this point, all I know is my poor mother does not deserve this. She does not deserve a life of dirty looks. You know what my mom has gone through just to get my brother and me to even get into college, let alone helping me go on this study abroad program!"

And then out of the blue we heard a gunshot. It seemed to echo off the volcano. It was crisp and clear. From a distance we saw Amox approaching in his truck, his shotgun poking through the driver's window. God had heard my prayers! Again, Amox fired another shot into the air. The bulls stopped moving towards us and all cocked their heads towards Amox. He let out several yells and fired the gun in the air one more time. The bulls then began to retreat, Ferdinand still with the red shirt hooked to his horn. Amox positioned his truck in between the bulls and us. We were probably half a football stadium's length from the bulls and his truck was about the same. The bulls snorted, turned, and ambled in the opposite direction, towards the volcano. Amox gestured for us to keep walking on the trail back towards the lodges. I could barely make out the distant silhouettes of the little buildings at that point, but felt so relieved to see them.

None of us could believe what had just happened. It was just like the movies! Amox waved at us and we waved back. He just kept gesturing and pointing us towards the lodge. Enrique gave him a thumbs-up. We saw that once the defeated group of bulls, led by Ferdinand, who was still sporting his new stylish red head garment, were almost out of sight, Amox got out of his truck and gathered all of our tattered belongings and put them in the satchel he wore around his chest. He then got back into the truck and bumpily made his way to us. He stopped the truck and gestured for us to get in. We all hopped in the truck. Enrique and José took the back and the rest of us sat up front with Amox. It truly was surreal.

We were still all somewhat in a state of pure shock. As the truck bumped along the trail we thanked him over and over for saving us from the bulls. He said he had seen them earlier in the day, and when he noticed them digging through our stuff he thought he had better keep watch, knowing we would be coming back that way. When we arrived at the lodge we all tumbled out of the truck.

"Well, looks like we will all be staying in the lodge tonight," Enrique laughed. I laughed to myself about how life works out sometimes. Those bulls saved me from having to spend the evening with "The Winker" (as I was now calling Javier), and maybe they saved Enrique, José, and Kelly from being eaten by a puma as well.

Chapter Seventeen

As we thanked Amox for all his help, his partner, Coaxoch, who looked much like Amox, emerged from the lodge. He too had long hair in a braid and wore pretty much the same attire as Amox. His eyes were a lighter shade of brown and he spoke less Spanish than Amox. His face was more weathered, and he appeared about ten years older than Amox. In Nahuatl, Amox explained to Coaxoch what happened with the bulls, and Coaxoch laughed a hearty laugh. His eyes became slits when he smiled and wrinkles formed at the corners of his eyes. His teeth were white as the snow on the top of Popo, and he exuded an amazing energy, as if he were some sort of animal, but a happy one. I hoped he would laugh again like that just so I could see his eyes turn into slits and the corners crinkle. Amox told us his name meant "Serpent Flower," and that was EXACTLY what I thought he looked like – a nice serpent.

"What does your name mean?" I asked Amox.

"'Amoxtli' means 'protector,'" he said, and the moment he said it we all broke out laughing.

"YOU ARE! You really are a protector!" Kelly said. Amox smiled modestly. He then said he would go out back to their ice chest and bring in some cold drinks. Coaxoch just sat and smiled at us, his eyes all squinty and crinkled.

Serpent Flower, that blew my mind. I wanted to ask him so many questions as well, like how he became a scientist, was he married, did he have kids. But we all just sat there smiling. Enrique pulled the bottle of pulque out of his bag and offered it to Coaxoch. Coaxoch chuckled again, showing off his white teeth, and gestured no thank you. Amox returned, bringing a pitcher of horchata with eight glasses full of ice.

As we drank the sweet horchatas I wanted so badly to ask if they would show us their lodge. I was so curious to see all the equipment used to monitor the volcano. My gut told me to leave well enough alone though. By then the sun was starting to go down and Enrique said we had better get the lodge set up and figure out who was sleeping where. Luckily his camp stove survived the "trampling of the bulls," as we were now calling it, and we still had at least some provisions left in the lodge to make dinner with.

I told everybody that I had brought a deck of cards, and Javier suggested we play a game of poker that night. We could use coins as chips, suggested Kelly. Enrique cooked up the food and we all drank wine and talked about how incredible the day was. The temperature had already dropped quite a bit, so we all bundled up in our clothes, putting layer over layer and huddling together.

"Wow, hace frío!" ("Wow, it is cold!") Kelly said.

"So, I guess strip poker is out of the question?" joked José, opening a bottle of wine. We all laughed. I caught Javier looking at me and he gave me a wink. I just smiled and tried to avoid eye contact at that point.

The night air grew colder and colder. José lit a joint, our last one, and we hoped that it would help us not think about the cold. The wine helped a bit, and by then we were into the game of poker. I caught on to the game with help from Kelly, who was actually the best player there.

She got really cocky about her prowess, and José began to actually become a bit of a bad loser. Every time Kelly would win she would say, "En tu cara, José! En tu cara!" ("In your face, José! In your face!") The first time it was funny. The second time he did not laugh as hard and at about the fifth time he told her to, "Callate la boca, mujer" ("Shut your mouth, woman"). It was clear it was time to go to bed because the wine was gone, José was getting crabby, Javier was actually almost asleep, and I think we were all totally beat from the day's adventure. So we made sure the camp stove was off and everybody got comfy in their sleeping bags. We all huddled next to each other trying to cultivate some group heat.

I lay there thinking about the amazing day and how God had really pulled through for me. I did promise him I was going to try to be a better person and to pray more. I also promised to be more grateful, and I decided to start listing all the things I was grateful for. I was grateful for God and for my family. For my health. I was grateful for education and for food and water and air to breathe. I was REALLY grateful for Amox for helping us out with the bulls. I was grateful for the bulls for making it impossible for Enrique, Kelly and José to camp. I went on and continued to mentally list all the things I was grateful for, and just as I was about to fall asleep, it started. Kelly began to snore.

It started as the Andy Griffith whistle, which was not too loud. I wondered if everybody else was asleep. Then I heard Enrique turn over in his sleeping bag.

"Callate, José!" ("Quiet, José!") he whispered, which made me giggle to myself. In the darkness of the lodge it was hard to tell where the noise was coming from, but when Kelly switched from the Andy Griffith to the Cement Truck, everybody besides her woke up with a start.

"Dije, callate, José!" ("I said, be quiet, José!") exclaimed Enrique one more time.

José sat up and said, "Dude, it's not me."

Then Enrique said, "Oh, sorry. I thought it was you." He turned and said, "*Shhhhh*, Javier, you are going to wake up the girls with your obnoxious snoring!"

"It's not me!" said Javier, sitting up groggily.

I could barely hold in my laughter at this point, and before being accused of snoring I pretended to wake up. I sat up acting like I was dumbfounded. "Hey... why is everybody awake?" I asked, stretching my arms and rubbing my eyes.

Kelly's Cement Truck then turned abruptly into the Delores Claiborne, and Javier said, "Crap, did one of the bulls get in here?" We all began to chuckle.

"Is that *Kelly* snoring?" Enrique asked in astonishment.

"Um, who else would it be?" asked José. "We are all accounted for."

Just then Kelly stopped snoring.

"Oh, good, she stopped," said Enrique. "It must be the cold air."

I laughed to myself. "Wishful thinking, there, Enriquito. I, too, have been fooled by this one before."

She remained quiet long enough for us all to lay back down. As soon as my head hit the pillow she started up again. "Ha!" I said in my head. "I called it. She is doing the old fake-a-roosky one." And all of a sudden all three guys sat up again with a start.

"Melissa," Enrique whispered.

"Um, yes," I said, sitting up.

"Does Kelly normally snore like this?"

Now, this was a tough one. I *soooooooo* badly wanted to scream out, "YES! EVERY G-DAMN NIGHT SHE SNORES LIKE THIS!" but I held back, thinking about what that would accomplish. Number one, it would only make her feel bad to know that I never said anything to her about it, but had I said anything to her it would have made her feel bad anyway – so it was a major Catch Twenty-two. Number two, I had made it this long and I had the extra key to the house, so in just a couple more weeks I would never have to say a word to her about it.

At the same time I did so badly want to tell them the different names of the snores, and how I have been sneaking into the house to sleep, and how difficult it has been, but something told me not to. Maybe God gave me some wisdom on this one because I decided to say, "Um… sometimes…."

Kelly's snore then broke into a whole new snore I had never heard. It literally sounded like a volcano erupting, with spits and spats here and there and then a really loud booming snore and then more spits and spats. This was SO hard, because humor had helped me survive the wrath of her snores, but now this… the Popo snore!

But before I said anything more, José said it for me. "It sounds like Popo is erupting! Everybody, quick, let's go wake up the scientists!" Everyone, including me, burst out laughing and I thought to myself, "God is good. God is great. God has a sense of humor!" I did not even need to say a word, it was not me teasing Kelly, it was Javier! I just sat there laughing along. It felt so good to laugh with other people about this. I figured Kelly would wake up at some point to our howling laughter but nope, she just kept on with the ol' Popo, sputtering and spattering in between what sound liked large spewings of hot lava.

"We should carry her back into the field and give the pumas a fright!" said Javier, and we all burst out laughing again.

"That is not nice, Javier," I said.

"Not nice? Listen to her!" he joked. "How do you sleep in the same room with her night after night? Is it like this all the time?"

I lied and said, "I think Enrique is right, it must be the cold air."

You see, this is one of those subtle rules of life again. Yes, the Bible says do not lie, but what if it causes more pain to someone to tell the truth than a lie? My mom taught me about something called "The Spirit of The Law" once, another subtle rule of life. There is the law, and then there is the spirit of the law. She gave the example of how even though it was illegal to hide Jews during the time of Hitler's reign, many religious people did it, and when the Nazis came knocking on doors asking if any Jews were hidden in the house, even the most religious person knew that in this case it was the spirit of the law that should be followed – and they would lie and say, "Nope, no Jews in here," and God did not punish them for lying, just as God would not punish me for saying that it was probably the cold air making Kelly snore when I knew damn well that the cold air had nothing to do with it. I would say, after having heard the newest snore, the

Popo, that the cold air definitely intensified her snoring. I did not think anything could get worse than the Delores Claiborne, I will tell you that much.

I also thought I should stick up for her more, even if she had snapped at me today about the camping thing. And as José and Javier went on and on about what the seismograph machine must be doing next door at the scientists' lab or how Kelly's snoring might actually set Popo off, I decided to pipe in and say, "It is not her fault, you guys," to which Enrique gave me a little help by adding, "Neither of you are Sleeping Beauties, either. I have heard you both snore."

Then after a pause he said, "Not as loud as Kelly, that is true, but…" and they all burst out laughing again. Suddenly Kelly stopped snoring, and for a moment I felt a dread that maybe she had been awake, listening. I was glad I at least tried to stick up for her.

But sure enough, a moment later she went right back into the Popo and the guys kept on suggesting that we take her outside.

"I need to sleep!" said José, now a bit irritated. Now they were getting the whole Kelly snoring effect. Yes, it was hilarious to come up with names and tease about it, but in the end, Kelly was the one who had the last laugh in this because she was sound asleep while the rest of us were MISERABLE! We had hiked all day, almost got taken out by a gang of bulls, it was growing colder by the minute, and here was Kelly, sleeping like a baby.

"Is there any more wine?" asked Javier.

"Nope" answered Enrique.

"I am going to go sleep in the car, then," Javier said. "Anybody want to join me?" he asked, looking at me.

As bad as Kelly's snoring was, and as good as a quiet place to sleep sounded, I said, "Um, I think I'll just wait it out in here. She will probably stop soon," I lied again.

Javier started to gather his stuff and José said he would go with him. As they packed up their stuff I said, "Hey, maybe you guys can go easy on her tomorrow about this? I mean, she can't really do anything about it, ya know?"

José said, "It may be better for her to know. I mean, listen to her for crying out loud. She may have something medically wrong with her that she should have taken care of."

Javier chuckled.

"No, I am serious," continued José. "I feel like it is my duty to tell her about it. In fact, if we could get a recording of her it would be even better. The scientists may want a copy to keep on file," he said and began to laugh.

"Just go easy on her," I said as they opened the door to leave. Javier did not wink at me as they left, instead he gave me a sullen look that had "are you sure?" Written all over it.

"*Ughhhh*... guys," I thought to myself. I said goodnight and tried to act as though I had not noticed his disappointment.

Chapter Eighteen

Enrique and I arranged our sleeping bags and he began to laugh, saying he could not believe such a small girl could make such a rumbling noise. I laughed too, and told him I had been having the same exact thought ever since Kelly and I had become roommates. We both shivered and wrapped ourselves up in our respective spots. I said that I did not realize it would be that cold.

"Aha!" he exclaimed as if he had just remembered something important. "Guess what I have that I forgot about? It may help us stay warm." I was at a loss. He then pulled the pulque out of his bag. "I still have half a bottle," he said with a big smile.

"Should we tell José and Javier about it?" I asked.

"Nah," he said, waving his hand at the door. "Let them fend for themselves for a bit."

I was relieved when he said that. "I agree. Hand it over, mister." He passed me the flask. I took a big drink and passed it back.

An hour later Kelly was still snoring and Enrique and I were laughing as she alternated between one snore and another. We had talked a bit about our families, me sharing with him how I thought the bulls were seeking revenge because my dad rode bulls in the rodeo, and him telling me that the first time he went fishing with his dad he fell in the fish pond and scared all the fish away. He laughed and said he smelled so much like fish that his dad suggested they just fry him up, put some lemon on him, and eat him. As we swapped stories we swapped the bottle of pulque.

I think the drink hit me (along with being tired, a little sun burnt, probably a bit dehydrated, and generally amped up from the day), because before I knew it I found myself smack in the middle of telling him the whole Kelly snoring story. She snored along as I told him how it began, and then naming them (he erupted into laughter when he found out she was currently doing the Cement Truck), and all about how I had been sneaking into the house and how hard it had been to not burst into complete hysterics while listening to them trying to figure out who was snoring. We were laughing so hard Enrique was almost hyperventilating. I made him promise not to tell anyone else, it had to be our secret. We pinky swore, and just as we were about to unlock pinky fingers he pulled me close to him and kissed me on the lips.

Now, THAT I was not expecting! I pulled back from him, showing him my surprise.

"I'm sorry, Melissa," he said as if even he was not expecting himself to have kissed me.

"No, no. You just surprised me," I said, pulling back a little more to show him I was not sure how I felt about it.

"Stupid me, stupid," he said shaking his head.

"No… no…" I said. Then, to try and lighten things up, I added, "I mean, you are kind of my brother – being that Elena is my house mother…." I laughed, and then he lightly laughed in return.

"That is true," he said.

"Now, if we were in Appalachia it might be a little different," I said, but he just looked at me in confusion. "Never mind," I said, realizing I was becoming more nervous by the minute.

"I do like spending time with you," he said. "You seem to have a calming energy."

"Thanks," I replied, trying to find words. "I just did not think you were interested in me… in that way."

And just as he was about to speak again, Kelly turned in her sleeping bag. She had been doing a very quiet version of the Andy Griffith – providing a little light romantic music for us, I guess you could say. She then let out a loud snort, waking herself up. We could not help laughing as she muttered sleepily, "Hey you guys… would you mind being quiet, I'm trying to sleep. If you are going to keep making so much noise could you go outside?"

We looked at each other and nearly burst out laughing. We decided to take the conversation outside, and as we stepped out we saw the sun just starting to make its ascent over Popo.

"Well," I said, "I have to say Kelly has the best and worst timing ever." Just as Enrique was about to reply, José opened the door to the truck and clumsily made his way to his feet. Javier opened the other door and did the same.

"Ellos también" ("Them too"), said Enrique with a chuckle, nodding at José and Javier as they yawned and stretched.

"Hey… perfect! Just in time for the sunrise," said José, stretching his arms and letting out a loud yawn. Javier glanced at me, said good morning, and asked how we slept. Enrique glanced at me with a twinkle in his eye.

"Good," I said. "She finally quieted down… eventually."

"Oh, that is good. Did you have to feed her and burp her before she quieted down, or did you have to sing her a lullaby, too?" joked Javier.

"Ha, ha, very funny," I said as we all huddled up to stay warm in the cold morning air.

Just then Kelly came stumbling out of the lodge, almost missing a step and falling. She was rubbing her eyes, her hair a mess. "Hey… why didn't anyone wake me for the sunrise?" she grumbled crankily. "I would have woken you guys up…" and JUST as she said that I gave José a look as if to say, "NOT A WORD, BUDDY! NOT A WORD." But sure enough, he and Javier broke out in hysterics.

"YOU would have woken US? YOU? US?" José laughed.

"Yes!" Kelly snapped, annoyed. "Why would you think I would have not woken you up?"

Before I could interject, José said, "Well, it is hard to wake people up that can't even fall asleep in the first place because of your snoring!" He and Javier chuckled. I looked at Enrique and could tell he was trying not to laugh.

"What!?" Kelly retorted. "I don't snore!" Javier and José once again burst out into hysterics.

"Oh, you snore, woman," said José. "Why do you think we slept in the truck?"

Kelly sat for a minute. I gave both José and Javier another look as if to say, "Let it go, guys."

Kelly puffed her chest a bit and said, "Oh, you're just mad because I beat you at poker, like, six times last night."

"What!?" laughed José. Before he could say anything more, in the same cocky manner as the previous night, she chided, "En tu CARA, José! EN TU CARA!" getting closer to his face with each word. José just stood there, speechless. She then kissed him on the cheek, patted his butt, and said, "Now go make me some coffee while I find a bush to pee in," and huffed off before anybody could say a word. I have to say, fifty percent of me loved the way she would get right up into people's faces, and fifty percent of me hated it, but at that moment, I had to admit I dug it.

"Lovely girl," said Javier sarcastically, watching as Kelly wandered off into the bushes.

"Yep, es un angel," added José as he started to make his way up the stairs of the lodge.

"You are not going to go make her coffee now, are you?" asked Javier with a laugh.

"I sure as hell am! I am kind of scared of what she will do if I don't," he said, opening the door to the lodge. "I am not even sure if she is a girl." The lodge door closed behind him. "In fact," we heard him say from inside the lodge, "I think she may be part werewolf, based on her howling." We all chuckled.

The coffee did the trick, and before we knew it we were all looking bright-eyed and bushy-tailed. We decided, though, that since the bulls had done away with about half our rations of food, and the previous night's sleep was less than a two-star rating, that we would call it a day early and head back while we were all still alive and kicking. We slipped a thank-you note under Amox's and Coaxoch's door along with a generous tip. The only person who got a good night's sleep was Kelly, who chatted the whole way home about how amazing the prior day had been and how she was not afraid for a minute of the bulls and how she was bummed they did not get to camp under the stars; but what a great night's sleep in that fresh mountain air!

José periodically rolled his eyes at Javier and vice versa while Enrique and I exchanged smirks. I was grateful nobody forced the snoring subject at this point. On the way home everybody except Kelly and Enrique (who was driving) fell asleep. Before I knew it we had dropped Javier and José off at their respective homes and were headed back to Elena's.

On the way back to Elena's, Enrique said the following weekend they would most likely go dancing again. He said he would love if we joined them, so we set plans to talk mid-week. I did not know if I should try to find a moment alone with Enrique or just wait to see what new developments might arise the next time I saw him.

Chapter Nineteen

As we unloaded our bags from Enrique's car, Elena came out to greet us. She asked how our trip had been. We all exchanged glances before Enrique piped up and said, "Muy bien, mama. Muy, muy hermosa la tierra y la naturaleza." ("Very good, mama. The land and nature were very beautiful.") If only we could have told her the whole truth! She kissed us all and said she was glad her girls and boy were back safe and sound. Again, we all shot each other looks as if to say, "So are we!"

Elena then told us she and a friend from work were going to see the movie *Titanic*, which had just opened in the theatres. She invited us to go along, and my first instinct was to say no, but then I thought it might be fun to go to a movie in Mexico, especially one starring Leonardo DiCaprio. I mean, really, what girl does not want to sit and watch Leonardo?

We were also told that going to see a movie was a good way to practice Spanish as they are generally dubbed from English to Spanish. Kelly was up for it, and even Enrique said he wanted to go, so we quickly dropped our bags in the cottage and all piled into Elena's car and headed to the movie theatre.

As we entered the lobby of the theatre a man greeted us. He was about Elena's age. He was shorter than Elena and had a sweetness to him, like a teddy bear. His light brown eyes began to dance the minute he saw Elena walk in the door. He was holding a flower, which he handed to Elena as he gave her a hug and a light kiss on the cheek. Elena blushed awkwardly, taking the flower and looking at Enrique with an almost embarrassed expression.

"Ah, que bonito, Ernesto, gracias," ("Ah, how beautiful, Ernesto, thank you,") she said. "Ernesto, esto es mi hijo, Enrique." ("Ernesto, this is my son, Enrique.")

"Ah, mucho gusto, he escuchado mucho de ti," ("Ah, nice to meet you, I have heard a lot about you,") said Ernesto as he and Enrique shook hands.

Poor Enrique looked as if he wanted to say, "Ahhh, that is interesting, because I have not heard *anything* about you. Nada. Zilcho." His response, however, was both polite and friendly. "Todo bien, espero!" ("All good, I hope!")

Ernesto chuckled. "Por supuesto! Por supuesto! Tu mama me dice que trabajas en la sector financiaero, ella siempre habla muy bien de ti." ("Of course! Of course! Your mama tells me you work in the financial industry. She always speaks very highly of you!")

Once again, it seemed like Enrique wanted to say, "Yep, yep, once again, gotta be honest, she has not said a peep about you, yet here you are, bringing her a flower." It is funny how grown men become very territorial about their mothers. Maybe it is even more pronounced in Mexico, where the term "mama's boy" is taken to a completely new level. I felt that as polite as Enrique was being, he was definitely exuding some kind of protective vibes which maybe I was the only one picking up on, because before anyone else could say a word, Kelly told Elena she should put the flower in her hair and proceeded to take it upon herself to do it for her. Kelly took the flower and then pulled a bobby pin out of her purse and wisped a lock of Elena's hair back, tucking the flower in.

"Ahhhhh, qué bonita!" Kelly exclaimed. I had to admit the flower was the perfect touch.

Elena blushed and Ernesto said with a chuckle, "Perfecto! Pues, esa tiene que ser tu estilista personal!" ("Perfect! So, this must be your personal stylist!") Kelly and I were both proud because we were able to understand what Ernesto was saying, and we all laughed, including Enrique.

"Estos son los estudiantes americanos que viven conmigo. Ellas son mis chicas, Kelly y Melissa" ("These are the American students that live with me. They are my girls, Kelly and Melissa"), she said, pulling us to her with her arms around each of our shoulders.

"Ah, sí mucho gusto" ("Oh, yes, nice to meet you"), Ernesto said.

"Mucho gusto también" ("Nice to meet you, too"), we replied at the same exact time. Again we all broke out laughing at our perfect synchronicity.

As we got in line for tickets, we chatted with Ernesto completely in Spanish. This was a turning point for both Kelly and me because we realized we were actually conversing in Spanish with a native speaker! Ernesto did not speak much English, so it was pretty much on us to put our skills to use! Elena told us that she and Ernesto had worked together for about five years. He had a management position at Macy's and often they would have lunch together. This seemed like news to Enrique, and I must say she had never said a word about Ernesto to Kelly or me, but one thing was clear – he had a thing for her! You could tell by the way he looked at her, and with the flower in her hair she lit up even more.

Before we went into the movie, Elena, Kelly and I used the restroom. I know Kelly was dying to interrogate Elena a bit about Ernesto, but there were so many women in the bathroom, it was hard to hear anything above the loud hand-dryers and flushing toilets. While washing my hands I caught a glimpse of Elena as she glanced at herself in the mirror wearing the flower. "Ah, sí, es bonito" ("Ah, yes, it is beautiful"), she said to herself with a pleased look. She then took out her lipstick and dabbed a little on her lips, complementing the red of the flower. Kelly then exited her stall and said that she thought Ernesto and Elena should sit next to each other and gave Elena a wink.

We all chuckled and Elena said, "Somos amigos, solo amigos! No sé por qué me trajo esta flor." ("We are friends, just friends! I don't know why he brought me this flower.") She then looked in the mirror one more time and it was obvious she was very, very pleased.

I looked at the flower in her hair and said, "Uh huh. Solo amigos?" with a laugh.

She chuckled, put her arms around us, and said, "Ah, mis hijas Americanas. Las voy a echar de menos muchisimo cuando salen." ("Ah, my American daughters. I am going to miss you so much when you leave.") It hit me that as much as Elena loved her Enriquito, she may have really loved to have a little girl (or two or three) as well. There was something very nurturing about how she said she would miss us.

When we met up with the guys it seemed like Enrique had loosened up a bit. They were both fans of soccer and were talking about how Ernesto had been to see the World Cup several times. Enrique was fascinated. When Ernesto saw Elena his eyes began to dance again. She blushed and he blushed and it was obvious Kelly wanted to make some remark like, "Oh, why don't you two just go get a room!" but she held back.

As we sat down in the theatre, Kelly made absolutely sure that Ernesto and Elena sat next to each other. She ushered us all in and sat at the end, plunking Enrique and I right next to each other as well. Little did Kelly know she was not only playing Cupid for Elena and Ernesto, but for Enrique and me as well. As we sat down I felt Enrique's knee touch mine and it brought me right back to the very first date I had ever been on – in eighth grade. I went to see *Gremlins 2* of all movies with a boy from my school, Joe Phillips, and it was apparent neither of us were ready to date. We were so awkward I think everybody, including the old guy who takes the tickets at the door, felt how nervous we both were.

I of course had some ridiculous late-eighties / early-nineties get-up on, including stone-washed Guess jeans rolled at the bottom and, I am sure, lip-gloss (which I learned later in life guys actually hate). Well, Joe really got into the movie, and I think he completely forgot about me as Gizmo the Gremlin took to the screen.

Yeah, that is what I was up against, a freakishly small guinea pig/bat-looking creature named Gizmo. So me and my stone washed jeans and shiny red lip-gloss took a clear second place to a little furry monster (voiced by none other than Howie Mandel, mind you), and I did not get one touch to the knee, no yawn move, nada. Nothing. Total disappointment.

So here I am, almost a decade later, sitting in a darkened movie theatre (in Mexico, mind you!) wondering if Enrique is going to do the yawn move on me, and as the movie starts, just as I am about to forget the whole idea all together, I feel his hand gently grab mine and I felt that same rush I felt way back in middle school on that first date. He squeezed it lightly and put it on his leg. I was at this point thinking about how good he smelled and about the kiss in the lodge and how we talked and laughed until the sun came up and then I squeezed his hand lightly to let him know I was good with the move he just put on me.

I had to laugh, wondering if the same thing was happening between Elena and Ernesto. Was Ernesto holding Elena's hand? At that moment I was so grateful for the part of Kelly that would just get right up in people's faces. I loved how she seized the moment and actually transformed what was somewhat of an awkward moment with Ernesto and the flower to a very sweet moment that may blossom into something more. I wished José were there for Kelly to hold hands with (after, of course, she had made him go and buy her a large popcorn and soda), but she seemed completely content sitting and watching as Leonardo charmed Kate Winslet into leaving the ridiculously boring elite class party on the top deck of the *Titanic* to go with him to where the real party was happening below.

Enrique's hand went from my hand to my knee and I was feeling all sorts of feelings at that moment. As Celine Dion belted out "My Heart Will Go On," I was pretty sure I was falling for him. I wished we were the only ones in the theatre and I could lean over and kiss him. Thankfully the credits started rolling before my mind went to other places, and as we exited the theatre I realized I was so engrossed in all my thoughts during the movie and Enrique's hand on my knee and mine on his – that it is a good thing it is a historical fact that the *Titanic* sank because had anyone asked me what the movie was about I would have had to BS my way out of the question.

On the way back to Elena's we hatched up a plan for dinner. The next day was Sunday, so we did not have to be up early. Kelly asked Enrique to call José and invite him too. Elena said she had wanted to make us pozole, and this was the perfect night for it. After dropping Elena and Ernesto at the house, where they were to start preparing the pozole, Enrique, Kelly and I drove to pick up José.

"Pozole," Enrique explained, "was made to be enjoyed on special occasions." He then went on to explain that pozole was a dish made of maize and carne. I looked back at Kelly, who was sitting in the back seat, to see how she felt about that, but either she was not listening or she did not care because she was engrossed in applying her mascara and primping up a bit before we stopped to pick up José. She had her compact mirror in one hand and a cigarette hanging out of her mouth. "Shit!" she exclaimed as we went over a bump and her mascara brush slipped.

Enrique went on to say that maize was a sacred plant for the Aztecs. In ancient times pozole was actually made from a mix of maize and human flesh from prisoners whose hearts were torn out in a ritual sacrifice to the Gods. The rest of the body was chopped up and cooked with the maize. I looked back at Kelly to see her reaction to this and nope, nothing. She was on to applying her blush.

"Wow, that is fascinating," I said. I really liked that Enrique was interested in the history and traditions of life. He was intelligent and knowledgeable, and damn he smelled good! I was not really into cologne, but he sure knew how to wear it!

"Did they really eat human flesh?" I asked, glancing back to see if that struck any nerves with Kelly, and still nope, she was adding the last final touches of lipstick.

"That is what scholars say," replied Enrique. "The meal was shared among the whole community as an act of religious communion."

"Wow," I said, remembering that I still did want to go to a Mexican church at some point, and I had not completely given up on getting Kelly to confession as I heard her swear for about the fifth time during that car ride alone.

"Could ya take it easy on the pot holes there, Enrique?" she griped. "I am trying to get ready back here." I shot Enrique a look and we both smiled. He finished his story about the pozole by explaining that after the Spanish Conquest, when cannibalism was banned, pork became the staple meat in pozole as it "tasted very similar," according to a Spanish priest.

He finished his historical narrative just as we arrived at José's house. José was waiting outside with a bottle of wine in hand. He jumped in and kissed Kelly on the cheek. "¿Cómo está mi reina?" ("How is my queen?"), he asked.

"I'd be a lot better had Enrique just kept that whole history of pozole story to himself. Geez, thanks a lot, Enriquito," she said, sounding genuinely disturbed.

"Oh, the human flesh thing?" asked José with a laugh.

"YES!" exclaimed Kelly. Enrique and I once again exchanged looks, and I laughed.

"So you WERE listening!?" I said, turning around.

"Duh, of course!" she snapped. "Just as I was sort of opening up to the idea of eating meat you had to go tell that story!"

We all chuckled. "I am never eating pork. Ever!" she said emphatically, making a face as though she had just downed a shot of strong whisky.

José leaned over and kissed her cheek. "My queen knows what she likes and knows what she doesn't like," he said with a smile.

Chapter Twenty

When we arrived at the house the pozole prep was under way. Elena and Ernesto were laughing as we entered, and right away Elena informed Kelly that she was making her her very own vegetarian pozole.

"Oh good, no human flesh in it, right?" said Kelly.

"Ahhhh! Enriquito told you the story of pozole," Elena chuckled. She pinched Kelly's cheeks and said, "My little vegetarian, you are so much trouble, but that is okay." Elena seemed more upbeat than I had seen her in a long time, and I noticed she was not smoking as much.

While she and Ernesto worked away in the kitchen, we set the table and opened the bottle of wine. Every now and again we could hear Elena let out a giggle or a laugh. Kelly and José went to the cottage to find some good music, and Enrique and I went out back to pick some flowers for the centerpiece of the table. We could still hear Elena and Ernesto laughing. Enrique was quiet as he knelt down to cut a few gardenias from the garden.

"I was not expecting her friend from work to be a man. I mean, she has lots of friends from work – all women, though." He was quiet again.

"Does it bother you?" I asked.

"No. I mean it is just strange because I only knew her to be with my dad. I am not sure another man, besides family or the plumber, has stepped inside this house besides my dad."

"That must be strange," I said. "She said in the bathroom at the theatre they are just friends though," I added. Then we heard Elena let out a really loud laugh.

"It is nice to hear her laugh like this, though," he admitted. "She has not laughed like that since my dad used to sweep her off her feet and make her dance with him in the kitchen."

We both had bundles of flowers in both our hands by this point. "Think we have enough?" I asked. He gestured for me to set them down on a bench facing the garden. We both sat down.

"Ha ha," he chuckled. "See over there…" he pointed to a pile of sticks about five feet tall resting against a wooden shed. "Those are all the walking sticks my dad used to bring home after hikes."

"Wow!" I exclaimed. "There must be almost a hundred of them."

"Ha ha," he laughed again. "Mi mama keeps telling me we need to get rid of them. She wants to plant a vegetable garden there. I just can't seem to get myself to remove them for her," he said, looking down at his hands.

There was an uncomfortable silence, but before it grew any more awkward Kelly and José came outside with four wine glasses and the bottle of wine.

"We must make a toast!" said Kelly as she set down the glasses on the bench and filled each glass with wine. We each took a glass.

"I'll start," said José. "To pozole!" he exclaimed. "Vegetarian pozole, of course," he added mischievously when Kelly shot a look at him.

"To Ferdinand the Bull!" said Kelly. We all laughed.

"To Popo!" I said.

Enrique paused and looked at the pile of walking sticks. "To the future!" he said, raising his glass. I gave him a look as if to say that I knew he was talking about letting his papa go, and we all clanked glasses.

"Yeeeeeehaaaaaawwww!" shouted José.

We all laughed and shouted out, "Yeeeeehaaaaw!"

"You know what we should do tonight?" Enrique asked the group. "Let's have a bonfire!" he said enthusiastically. I looked at him and then at the pile of his dad's walking sticks.

"Yes! Un fuego!" ("Yes! A fire!") chimed Kelly.

"We never got to have one at Popo, so let's do it here!" declared Enrique. "We have all that firewood," he said, pointing to the pile of sticks, "and it is a perfect night for one."

So, it was decided. We would have a fire that night, and Enrique would maybe have some much needed closure with his papa. We each helped out by taking bundles of the sticks and putting them into the fire pit. Enrique then told me that he wanted to pick out a couple to save. We chose several beautiful ones and set them aside and then, as the sun had almost set, Elena called us in for dinner.

It was, in one word, delicioso. As we ate, Ernesto told us that pozole is a well-known cure for hangovers and is often eaten in the wee hours of the morning in order to prevent a hangover from even occurring.

"Y, si ese es el caso ¿por qué no abrimos otra botella de vino?" ("And if that is the case why don't we open another bottle of wine?") said Enrique as he got up to go get another bottle. Elena told us that pozole was relatively easy to make – just, pork, maize, garlic, cumin, salt and water. She garnished the soup with cabbage, shredded onion, limes, avocado and cilantro, making it a medley to all the taste buds.

I was astonished by the freshness and cleanliness of the food I ate in Mexico. It was pure and clean – not processed like much of the food we eat in the United States. In Mexico, and in other countries I have been to in Latin America and Europe since, it seems like food is more of a medicine for the body as opposed to a poison. Food is eaten to prevent heart disease as opposed to causing it. I also noticed that ever since returning from Mexico I always get a kick out of the difference between real Mexican food and your Americanized Mexican food. I guess that is another reason why it is so important to break out and travel. One may think they are eating what people eat in Mexico, but unless you go there and taste it with your own mouth, you will never know!

As Elena, Ernesto and I cleaned up the table, Kelly and the men went outside and lit the fire. Elena then prepared some chocolate caliente and galletas (hot chocolate and cookies) and we took the tray and a small table out to the fire pit. Elena and Ernesto said that the fire was for "los jovenes" ("the youngsters") and they preferred to stay in and finish cleaning up.

Before we said goodnight, Ernesto said that he had invited Elena to go to Teotihuacan (pronounced Tay-Oh-Tee-Wa-Con) the following day. We had learned in one of our classes that Teotihuacan is a pre-Columbian Mesoamerican city located in the Basin of Mexico about thirty miles northeast of Mexico City. It is in this city that one will find the amazing Mesoamerican pyramids built in the pre-Columbian Americas.

Our teachers recommended going if we had the chance, and so we agreed we would go as well – that is, if the pozole trick really worked and we were not too hung over from the wine. I had to admit I was still sore from the long hike the prior day, but I was nevertheless feeling up for the adventure. It hit me that we only had one more week left of the program that night.

José passed on the last bit of wine as it was handed around, saying he was still recovering from the hike as well and wanted to be well hydrated for the pyramids. Then he and Kelly decided to take a walk to the cottage to bring out a pitcher of water.

Enrique and I sat under the moon and stars and watched his father's walking sticks turn into orange flits of fire and black and white ash. I looked at Enrique and said, "A tu papa" ("To your dad"). I held my glass up and took the last sip of my wine and turned to him. He pulled me in for a kiss, and we sat silhouetted by the fire, kissing as we listened to the cracking fire.

He pulled back, paused, and said, "You are leaving in a week."

"I know," I said.

"Any chance you can prolong your stay?" he asked, and added a little chuckle to lighten up the conversation. I had not considered that option up until that point, and before I completely dismissed the idea I thought about it. I had signed up for summer classes at the University of

Minnesota – but what better way to keep learning and practicing my Spanish than by staying in a country where it is spoken.

"Hmmm…" I said. "I had not considered that."

We began to kiss more and he pulled me in closer. Then my gut kicked in along with the part of my brain that generally helps me through decisions like this. In my heart I knew I barely had spent any time with Enrique. Sure we survived a night of Kelly's snoring together, which is a bond beyond saying wedding vows as far as I am concerned, and I do think he needed a shoulder to lean on when it came to seeing his mom with potentially a new man in her life; and lastly, I knew he was one hell of a dancer and a kisser – but I also felt in my gut that I did need to carry on with my own path. If we were meant to be, love would win in the end.

It is funny how our emotions can toy with us. Just hours before, while sitting in the movie theatre holding Enrique's hand, I felt I was really falling for him. Of course we did have Celine belting out in the background and Leonardo and Kate falling in love on the big screen and the love birds, Elena and Ernesto, sitting right next to us, so I went easy on myself. As we continued kissing, I thought about how I could tell him that as much as he made my heart pound, I knew I had to go back to Minnesota and stick to my own path for the time being. I had already signed up for summer classes – all Spanish courses – and I had also re-declared my major one more time (haha!).

As we pulled away, before I even needed to say anything, he took my hand and said, "I know you have to go back. But always remember, you have a family here in Cuernavaca, too."

I hugged him and told him he also had one in Minnesota. "If you are ever crazy enough to visit in the winter, I will take you ice skating and show you my spinning skills," I told him. We both laughed, and just then we heard José and Kelly approaching. We all watched as the fire dimmed.

Enrique looked at his watch. "Okay, if we want to have enough energy for the pyramids, we had better get going, José," he said. I think we were all tired from the day, and some of us from the lack of sleep the prior night. We said our "buenas noches" to one another and planned to meet in the morning. That night I fell so soundly asleep I did not hear a peep from Kelly. I knew I had made a wise decision about not staying in Mexico. My instincts told me I would be back again when the time was right.

The following morning we woke up bright and early, ready for our trip to the pyramids. We were told to bring lots of water since it would be hot on the hike. We wore good shoes and of course brought our cameras and a little bit of money for souvenirs. We drove in two cars, "los jovenes" in one and Ernesto and Elena in the other. On the way we sipped on coffee José had brought. It was Mexican coffee. I had had it several times and fell in love with it more and more each time I drank it. José said it was easy to make – just a combination of sugar, coffee, cinnamon, cloves and vanilla. It was like dessert in the morning.

Kelly took out her guidebook and began to read us a little about the history of our destination for that day. "'Teotihuacan was one of the largest urban centers in the ancient world, with a population of perhaps 125,000 or more,'" she read.

"Wow, only 125,000 people? I think New York City alone has something like eight million people," I said.

Kelly went on to read, "'At its peak, Teotihuacan encompassed an urban core of about eight square miles with a population estimated at more than 100,000 people. Its influence was felt throughout central Mexico and as far south as Guatemala. The city was organized using a grid plan, many people living in what scholars refer to as 'apartment compounds' containing multiple families.'"

"Ha ha, sure sounds like New York City," I quipped.

She finished with telling us that the name Teotihuacan was given by the Nahuatl-speaking Aztecs centuries after the fall of the city. The term means the "birthplace of the gods."

"Perfecto," said José. "Porque tú eres mi diosa, mi amor" ("Perfect, because you are my goddess, my love"), he said, and then he kissed Kelly on the cheek. Enrique gave me a look and rolled his eyes with a smirk.

When we arrived at the city it was much like when we had arrived at Popocatépetl. The immensity of the structures before us made me feel like an ant in the middle of a metropolis. We pulled in next to Ernesto and Elena's car, and after making sure we had all the necessities we would need for what we were told would be about a three-hour adventure, we decided to begin with a group photo before setting off on our tour. Kelly insisted that Ernesto and Elena be photographed – just the two of them. I had to admit they were pretty adorable as a couple. This turned into a whole photo shoot where we then took all sorts of pictures starting with just the girls, then just the guys, then just Kelly and I, then Kelly and José, then José and Enrique and so forth and finally ending with Enrique and I. We all laughed as we rotated in and out of the shots.

Upon approaching the ruins we decided to join a tour group so we could learn more. Yes, we felt like cattle being herded around, but sometimes that is okay, just make sure you have a spot in the front so you can hear! It was fascinating to see all the visitors, and I could see little groups of tourists huddled up around interpreters who were translating into different languages. I thought it would be interesting to be an interpreter as I watched them switch among the various languages. Maybe someday I would do some interpreting, I remember thinking to myself.

We learned that what we were first approaching was called the "Avenida de los Muertos" ("The Avenue of the Dead") and the towering Pyramids of the Sun and the Moon. Our tour guide explained that what we were witnessing were some of largest ancient pyramids in the world. According to legend, it was here where the gods gathered to plan the creation of man. As we kept walking I imagined what it would have been like to have actually lived there when it was a live city full of its original inhabitants. The thought that people constructed these pyramids just amazed me. The ingenuity it must have taken to design and build such immense structures out of stone was mind blowing.

We began to climb the Pyramid of the Sun. Ernesto and Elena decided to not venture on the climb, but rather take pictures and relax at the bottom. On the way up the tour guide told us that construction of Teotihuacán commenced around 300 B.C., with the Pyramid of the Sun built by 150 B.C. As we climbed I took notice that it was not only groups of tourists climbing the massive pyramid but locals as well. I saw a lot of families and groups of teenagers. I could mostly tell the difference between the tourists and the locals by the way people dressed. Tourists always tend to sport white tennis shoes, visors, and fanny packs and just have a "touristy air" about them, while the people from Mexico were dressed in more formal attire, as if they had just come from church (which they most likely had).

To be honest, I noticed that the people from Mexico tended to dress up more in general. The women were more made up and would dress up just to go out to the store (as opposed to many Americans who can be spotted just about anywhere, including church, sporting sweat pants, track suits, jeans, and frumpy tee shirts and sweat shirts). Not Mexicans though. There are parts of Minneapolis and St. Paul, Minnesota, where many Latino's live – primarily people from Mexico. I used to love going there on Sundays just to see the people out in their Sunday get-ups. The men would wear cowboy hats, button down shirts with boleros and handkerchiefs around their necks, and steel-toed boots, and the women would look like they were ready to attend a wedding. I just loved it. In my opinion they bring such color and life to a state that needs some flare.

I had to laugh, though, when I saw a couple ahead of us who appeared to be from Mexico (because of their dressy attire and their dark hair and skin) climbing the pyramid. The man was okay, but the woman, who for some reason thought it would be fine to wear five-inch high red heels and a skin tight red dress as she hiked one of the largest pyramids in the whole world, looked like she was in pure misery – go figure. It seemed at first like she was trying to act like she was fine climbing in her red stilettos, but every now and again she would turn on one of her ankles, almost falling and pulling down her date along with her. At first it seemed like he would comfort her and help her up, but after about the third time it looked as though he was gesturing for her to take them off.

I have to say, this was one of those moments you just wonder about the I.Q. of someone who woke up the morning they were set to hike up one of the largest pyramids in the world and most likely had trouble deciding whether to wear black stilettos or red ones, but alas, decided on the red ones because they looked cuter with the red skin-tight dress she was set on wearing. What in Heaven's name the gods, who had gathered at this very pyramid to plan the creation of man, must have been thinking as they looked down on this ridiculous spectacle? I bet they were thinking, "Crap! We did a half-assed job with some of these morons!" or, "Boy, have people become stupider or what? What a disappointment, I mean, really!" To think that at one point in time people were so intelligent they created, with their bare hands mind you, some of the most amazing wonders of the world; then fast-forward to today and this is what is going on?

I mean, this poor woman had blisters the size of nickels on her feet by the time we passed them, and that stone we were climbing on was hot and only getting hotter. It was not even ten a.m. yet. I felt especially bad for the poor schmuck who was with her because he was probably going to have to carry her at some point – and here is the kicker: she was not the only woman I saw wearing heels and a tight dress. There were a number of them, and they all looked ridiculous.

I then realized that I was missing out on some of the most fascinating scenery in the world because I was fixated on counting how many women I saw in heels and how eventually the heels would come off; and for one lucky woman, I kid you not, I saw her faithful mate sit down, take off his shoes and socks, and then give the miserable soul rubbing her feet next to him his very own socks so she could put them on and walk without burning her sore, blistered, bunion-ridden feet.

Then, eventually, the poor sockless man began walking funny because apparently socks serve a purpose when hiking in ninety-degree weather – they help prevent blisters. I felt like I was observing primates in the fields of Africa for crying out loud. So now both of these poor souls were miserable, and they still had to make their way back down the steps they had climbed. They eventually made it to the bottom, but still had to walk the distance to the parking lot, which was a mild trek in itself. I wondered if the entrance was called "The Avenue of The Dead" because all one would see on the way out would be men hobbling to their cars while carrying their fallen lovers over their shoulders.

HA! I guess the North American tourists wearing bright white athletic shoes and pure white socks weren't entirely stupid after all. So, once again, I most likely missed out on some fascinating facts as we completed the hike because I was so entranced by the whole hiking-with-heels thing, but what are you gonna do?

At the bottom of the pyramid we met up with Ernesto and Elena again, who said they enjoyed watching us appear to grow smaller and smaller as we ascended the great pyramid and then get bigger as we came back down. We laughed, and they asked if we were hungry. We had packed a picnic lunch and decided to find a spot to sit down and eat. I kept the heel story to myself because, honestly, I was pretty winded during the whole hike, and it took me a bit to recover my energy once we got to the bottom. Nobody else mentioned it, so I decided to keep it to myself. To this day, whenever I see red heels I think of that hike!

Chapter Twenty One

When we returned to Elena's house that afternoon I realized how tired I was and how it seemed like we had visited Popo a week prior as opposed to a couple of days. I felt like I had been on a whirlwind adventure since we left for the volcano. We said good-bye to Enrique and José, making plans to see them the following weekend. Elena invited us in for dinner, but I was so exhausted I told her I would pass and ended up falling asleep at seven that night. The following week we had our final exams so I wanted to be sure to be well rested. I must have been really knocked out because I am not sure if Kelly snored or not. All I know is that I woke the following morning to my alarm clock and the sound of birds singing. Kelly had already awakened and showered.

The day flew by as we started the process of turning in our final papers and preparing for the end of the program. We brought our last load of laundry that day, and as we walked from the bus stop to our school carrying our heavy laundry bags it hit me how much I was going to miss the routine I had become accustomed to, even if it did involve sneaking into the house each night to avoid putting a pillow over Kelly's face. Now that there was only one week left, I was able laugh to myself at the whole thing, and I was happy in the end I stuck it out and did not switch living situations. Kelly seemed extra quiet that day, and I wondered if she was realizing she was going to miss it too. She and José had also become pretty close, and the fact that even after hearing her Delores Claiborne he still called her his queen made me wonder if what I was witnessing between José and Kelly was what true love really looks like.

On our way home on the bus Kelly was still quiet. Just as I was about to ask her if she needed to talk about something she turned to me and said, "I am staying in Mexico longer. I am not ready to go back yet."

It seemed as though she must have been holding it in all day because she blurted it out in one breath and was looking at me with an expression that that said she was ready to defend her point, as if I was going to try to talk her out of it.

"Girl! I am so happy for you!" I said genuinely. I truly was happy for her, and when she said it, it just felt right hearing it. She told me how she wanted to stay for another semester, and in between she was planning to travel with José. I truly was happy for her, and I knew that José and Elena would both be ecstatic.

I hugged her and told her that I expected postcards and letters, and I told her that I could send her anything she was missing from the States. She assured me she would make a list for me. We chuckled, and then I turned to her. "You are not staying just to make sure Elena and Ernesto become a thing?" I asked.

"Well…" she said with a smirk, "it is on my list of things to do; that, and convincing Alita that chicken IS ACTUALLY MEAT!"

We both burst out laughing. "Yeah, well, good luck with that one!" I said. "I think Elena and Ernesto will get married long before you can convince Alita that chicken is meat."

We laughed the rest of the way home as I told her about my observation of the high heels at the pyramid. She confessed she was so distracted by making her big decision and by José (who I did notice was attached to her like a puppy dog) that she did not even notice the heels. I made her promise she would go back at some point and just sit and watch for heels. She laughed and promised that she would take pictures and send them my way. She requested that in exchange, upon returning to Minnesota I take pictures of the overly exuberant students who wear shorts the first day the temperature creeps up to fifty degrees.

Inevitably each spring there were always a number of girls, generally freshmen, who would decide to wear their Daisy Dukes and show off their blindingly white legs just because the temperature was above freezing for the first time in five months, and they looked pretty much as ridiculous as the women sporting heels at the pyramids. Fifty degrees is still cold enough to cause goosebumps and blotchy red skin, so essentially they'd end up looking like blotchy chickens wearing really short shorts – and that is not good for anybody to have to witness! I agreed to be camera-ready for any photo-ops, and we promised to try and write only in Spanish.

During dinner Kelly shared her news with Elena, and Elena almost had tears in her eyes she was so happy. She then looked at me and said, "And as for, you I understand you will keep learning Spanish when you return to Minnesota – so you must come back and visit. Promise?" she said as she put up her little finger.

I laughed and linked my pinky with hers. "I pinky swear," I said, and she pulled me in and kissed my cheek.

"I wish you were staying too, but I am so happy at least one of my girls will be staying," she said, pinching Kelly's cheek.

Alita came out of the kitchen with our dinner plates, and when Elena announced that they would only be losing one of us, Alita had a look of disappointment when she found out it was not Kelly. As much as she smiled and nodded her head that she was happy, you could tell she was frankly annoyed. Since the whole pozole incident Kelly was back on her strictly vegetarian diet, making Alita's job more challenging than she preferred. I guess if you had been under the impression that chicken is not meat for seventy years it would be hard to change your thinking overnight. I decided at that moment one of the first things I would send my Mexican family would be a vegetarian cookbook.

The following day our school had one last excursion planned for us. We were going to visit Xochimilco (pronounced, zochi-milko in Nahuatl), meaning "place of the flowers" or the "floating gardens." We were allowed to invite our respective host families on the excursion as part of the conclusion of the program. Unfortunately neither Elena nor Enrique were able to take time off work, but José was available so he joined us that day.

As we headed to the south of Mexico City where the gardens are located, our tour leader explained that in pre-Hispanic Mexico, in the valley where Mexico City is currently situated, was a lake called Lago Texcoco, which has long-since been drained. Many years before the Spanish arrived the Aztecs dug a number of canals, the sediment and mud from which they piled on the ground around them. Over time these formations of land transformed into what look like floating islands, and that is how they received the name "floating gardens."

Upon our arrival at the floating gardens we saw from a distance that the canals were full of what are called trajineras (trah-hee-ner-as), or flat boats. These flat boats are used to transport locals and tourists along the canals, much like the gondolas in Venice, Italy. They are as colorful as Frida Kahlo's blue house – painted with bright colors and decorated with colored flowers painted on them. About two thousand of these traijineras float through the canals daily. In the past, we learned, they were decorated with real flowers, but because real flowers can be so expensive the boats are just painted nowadays.

What we learned next adds to the number of reasons why I think it is important to travel and break away from the USDA approved herd many North Americans seem to roam in and get off the grid a bit. It also may serve as an interesting conversation piece when out with friends (or strangers for that matter). The "chalupa," believe it or not, isn't just some taco type thing served at Taco Bell. A chalupa is also a boat that travels along the canals through the floating gardens. It is very similar to the trajinera, only it is smaller than the trajineras and is commonly called a "decorated canoe" rather than a flat boat. Instead of transporting tourists and locals, they are used to transport vendors selling everything from drinks and food to art and handicrafts to the guests on the trajineras – like floating wait stations in a sense. Actually, to be more accurate, traveling down the canals was almost like going to a farmers' market on water.

Not only could one enjoy the food, drink and arts and crafts as they floated down the canals, but there was also music. We saw boats with Mariachi bands serenading passengers on trajineras for a small fee. José said he would make sure Kelly was serenaded, and then told me he would make sure I was not left out so not to worry. I had no idea what a spectacular sight we had in store for us on the way to the gardens and feel like this is another reason to add to the list as to why people should take that flight or boat or train to a place they have never been. You just cannot imagine how you may be surprised. Little did I know that a chalupa was something far more amazing than a meat-filled taco shell served from a fast food joint.

As we floated along, while being serenaded not once, not twice, but three times (after José made sure Kelly and I were both serenaded we made sure he was serenaded as well), we admired all that was happening on the banks of the canals as well as in them. Normal life was going on as usual for the locals who lived along the canals. We saw people working in their shops, kids diving into the canals to cool off from the sun, and people working in the yards of their houses. There seemed to be an air of true joy in the people as they went about their business, waving occasionally to one another as we floated along the festive waters.

We took pictures of the sights and enjoyed different types of food and drinks when the chalupas approached us. When we needed to, we could request to stop off at any point and walk around the banks on foot and then pick up another trajinera when we were ready to float some more. We set a meeting point and time with the excursion leader and other students, and after a relaxing four-hour journey we were back on the bus to head home.

After leaving the canals I knew I had absolutely contracted what is known as the "travel bug." Maybe it was something in the waters of those canals, maybe I had contracted it the moment I stepped off the plane in Mexico and got a good, strong smell of the warm, exotic air. At that point I definitely wanted to see the canals of Venice, Italy, not to mention the Amazon River in South America, the Seine in France and the Rhine in Germany. I looked at Kelly, her head resting on José's shoulder as we bumped along on the way, hearing her do a very, very quiet Andy Griffith while José's head rested on hers. Both of them were sleeping with what appeared to be smiles on their faces. Because it was late in the evening we were all dropped off directly at our homes.

That night Kelly stayed at José's house, leaving me plenty of time to start packing and studying for my final exams. As I alternated between packing and quizzing myself on vocabulary words, I realized that maybe I had not fallen in love with a Latin lover while in Mexico, but I had fallen in love with traveling. As I packed my belongings I knew that I might meet many Enriques through my future travels, but until I found true love like José and Kelly had found, I had to keep on my path of new discoveries, like what the real meaning of a "chalupa" is.

The following day I had my first set of exams. I felt really happy walking out of my classes, feeling confident I had done well. I knew at that point that I would not switch majors again. Spanish was it. Kelly came home that day, and on the bus ride she told me how she really felt like she was falling for José. She said they stayed up late talking and he had helped her study for exams, and they began to plan where they were going to travel to over the summer. They talked about traveling down to Zihuatanejo with Elena and Enrique to revisit the spot where Elena and Enrique Sr. spent their honeymoon. We looked at the guidebook and I have to say I was slightly tempted, but knew I would be back someday.

The following day was our final Friday and the last day of the program. The school planned a special dinner, graduation ceremony and dance for the students and school staff for the following evening, and my flight was set to leave on Sunday. After turning in our final papers and projects and tying up loose ends, Kelly and I took our last bus ride home together. I think we were each feeling both a mixture of relief that we had made it through the program and sadness that it was over with. I told her that I had already started looking into other programs the University offered. There was one that took students to Spain and another to Venezuela. I was leaning towards Spain because I had always wanted to go to Europe.

"Maybe we should meet up in Spain?" Kelly said with a smile.

"Quizás" ("Maybe"), I replied with a smile. "Imagine the bulls we would encounter there," I said, and we both laughed.

"At least there are no volcanoes in Spain," she said, and we both laughed. That evening I finished most of my packing while Kelly read more about Zihuatanejo. We had our final dinner with Elena. Alita made Mexican lasagna – one pan was meatless for Kelly and ours had beef in it. Alita must have figured out that she had better surrender to Kelly because she was going to have to deal with her for at least a couple more months if not longer.

Kelly and I stayed up late that night. We brought a bottle of wine to the balcony and made a toast to each other. We laughed about everything from the first dinner we had with Alita denying that chicken was meat, to the first night out with Enrique and the boys, to our encounter with Ferdinand the Bull. We were rolling in laughter by the time we began to reminisce about my "chicken pox scare" and her "pregnancy scare." I truly was going to miss her. We drank the whole bottle of wine, and by the time my head hit the sack even the Popo could not wake me.

The following day we spent with Elena helping her plant her tomato garden where Enrique Sr.'s old walking stick collection had been. Ernesto came over with some good potting soil, and when we finished we had a late afternoon picnic lunch while admiring the new garden. After lunch Kelly and I got ready for the graduation ceremony. We all left together and arrived at the school, which was decorated with lights and flowers and ribbons. The ceremony commenced right on time. As I watched everybody approach the stage to receive their certificates it hit me how fast the program actually had flown by. I watched one student, the guy who had trouble with the word "enfocar," take his certificate and chuckled, thinking back to that day in class. He had a big smile on his face and waved his certificate in the air. He got a big cheer. As Kelly and I approached the stage and received our certificates we heard a loud "Yeeeehaw!" and a bunch of whistling, which caused a rumble of laughter in the room.

After the dinner and ceremony, the staff cleared the tables and lowered the lights for the dance. I was so happy I had had a chance to practice the salsa with Enrique and Javier because the DJ played mostly salsa. I showed off my spinning and Enrique showed me a couple more moves. José and Kelly definitely had a connection because they were magic on the dance floor. Javier gave me a hug when I saw him, and before I knew it he was dancing with a girl who I could tell was probably thinking, "Wow, he is like a Mexican version of Ryan Gosling...." I watched as he would wink at her while they danced and she was soaking it all in.

I watched as Ernesto and Elena danced. She was amazing to say the least. I could just picture her back in the day with Enrique Sr. dancing in the kitchen. I am sure he was happy to see her dancing again, and I am sure he was smiling down on the tomato garden as well. We danced the night away, switching partners and taking photos.

By the end of the dance I was pretty exhausted. It had been a full day of exams, turning in final papers and tying up loose ends. My flight was set for Sunday afternoon, and after a number of dances Enrique said one more time, "You suuuuuure about going back? Kelly is staying. Just imagine the trouble we could all get into this summer...."

"Yes, I know," I smiled. "That is one of the reasons I think it is best I go back," I said with a little wink. "I can ONLY imagine after the adventures we have already had!"

He gave me one last spin and a little dip and said, "Well, then I must come to you and see you do your spins on ice skates."

He pulled me up and gave me a little kiss on the cheek. It seemed like he was fishing for more. I kissed him back on the cheek and told him I would be warming up the ice for him, and we hugged one last time.

We arrived at Elena's at about ten, and luckily I had pretty much completely packed that afternoon because I was exhausted once again from all the day's festivities. Kelly was tired as well, and so after showering we both fell into our little beds in our perfect cottage in our perfect paradise and said good night to each other for the last time. I lay there for a few minutes, and as I listened to the warm Mexican breeze, feeling it wafting through our little window, I began wondering if I had made the right decision to go back. For a moment I feared that maybe once I got back to Minnesota I would lose the "travel bug" and end up never traveling again. What if this was a once in a lifetime chance?

Then I started getting a bit worked up. Had I thought this through completely? What if I ended up married in five years with three kids and some dopey husband who was more into his Foreman grill and playing fantasy football with his friends than really living life while I essentially raised the kids and worked some hideous job that I hated? And of course it would be just my luck to have all boys who turned out just like their father and got all into fantasy football and video games and barbequing on the ol' Foreman and never had any interest in seeing the world either, and suddenly I was in a panic. By forty my life would be over, my husband would most likely be having an affair – or at least contemplating the idea, my kids would hate me and I would have never taken that gondola ride in the canals of Venice, Italy. There was still time to change my plans, I thought, and I started planning exactly what I would say to my family and friends back home. It was not too late.

And just as I was about to get up and start unpacking my suitcase, it began. Kelly began a mixture of the Popo and the Delores Claiborne, and I KNEW it was God telling me I was making the right decision to go home, and that this was only the beginning of my adventures abroad. He could not have sent a clearer sign, because Kelly was on fire that night. She seemed to be doing a hybrid of all her various snores, much like the grand finale of a Fourth of July fireworks display, making it ABUNDANTLY clear that one more night with her and I REALLY might do something I'd regret. I thanked God for squashing my doubts so speedily and effectively.

Kelly kept up with the snoring all night. At least I would sleep well on the plane, I reasoned, and I watched as the sun came up through our window, chuckling as I listened to her snore. "THIS I will not miss," I thought to myself.

After waking and getting ready we had our last breakfast together, and Alita brought out some Mexican coffee as a going away treat. Elena drove me to the airport. Kelly accompanied us. Sure enough, although I was all glassy-eyed from lack of sleep, Kelly went on and on about how well she slept and asked if I was TOTALLY sure about my decision. I chuckled, yawned and said, "Absolutamente" ("Absolutely").

As the plane took off I waved from the window. I was not sure if Kelly or Elena could even see me, but figured it could not hurt. After a little light chitchat with the man sitting next to me, he asked if I was returning home to the States for good.

"No sir," I said. "I am just making a pit stop there… to refuel, you could say." The plane took off and the sound of the engines made my heart pound. This was only the beginning….

About the Author

Merideth Rose Cleary holds a Masters Degree in Spanish from Middlebury College as well as a Bachelors Degree in Spanish from the University of Minnesota, where she graduated Phi Beta Kappa in 2000. During her undergrad and graduate studies she participated in three study abroad programs.

She currently lives on the North Shore of Oahu, Hawaii, where she is a certified yoga instructor and is currently writing her second novella in the *Abroad* series; *ABROAD: Toledo, Spain.*

Made in the USA
Charleston, SC
15 January 2015